A PIECE OF HEAVEN

SHARON DENNIS WYETH

Alfred A. Knopf ✎ New York

THIS IS A BORZOI BOOK PUBLISHED BY ALFRED A. KNOPF

Text copyright © 2001 by Sharon Dennis Wyeth
Jacket illustration © 2001 by Allen Garns

www.randomhouse.com/kids

KNOPF, BORZOI BOOKS, and the colophon are registered trademarks of
Random House, Inc.

Library of Congress Cataloging-in-Publication Data
Wyeth, Sharon Dennis.
A piece of heaven / by Sharon Dennis Wyeth.
p. cm.
Summary: Thirteen-year-old Haley holds her life together with the help of good
people after her mother suffers a nervous breakdown and her brother is arrested.
ISBN 0-679-88535-8 (trade) — ISBN 0-679-98535-2 (lib. bdg.)
[1. Family problems—Fiction. 2. Mother and child—Fiction.
3. Emotional problems—Fiction. 4. Brothers and sisters—Fiction.
5. Afro-Americans—Fiction.] I. Title.
PZ7.W9746 Pi 2001
[Fic]—dc21   00-062930

Printed in the United States of America

January 2001

10   9   8   7   6   5   4   3   2   1

This book is dedicated to the friendship and wisdom of

Graham and Madeleine Bernard

Eunice Jackson

Thelma Markowitz

Marian Rich

Dr. M. Jerry Weiss and Helen Weiss

Sims and Georgia Wyeth

ACKNOWLEDGMENTS

Many thanks to my editor, Andrea Cascardi. Her comments throughout the phases of A *Piece of Heaven* provided a well of encouragement and insight. I am grateful as well to my agent, Robin Rue, for her enthusiasm and for reading the manuscript in earlier drafts. Georgia Wyeth, my daughter, has read my works-in-progress since the age of five! I always await her response eagerly, because of the truth it provides. My husband, Sims Wyeth, continues to be steadfast and loving in his support.

Conversations I had with Carol Smith-Njiiri, Senior Vice President of Family and Children Services of HeartShare Human Services of New York, helped immeasurably, as did the talk I had with Terry McKeon, Senior Vice President of Developmental Disabilities. Part of the aim of the multi-service agency where Mrs. Smith-Njiiri and Mr. McKeon work is to find ways to help children who have lost their families and homes or who are in need of other support. I hope that A *Piece of Heaven* pays tribute in a small way to the resilience and bravery of such young people and to the dedication of those who reach out to them.

Ever since I learned to read, fairy tales have been a mainstay for me. While I was writing *A Piece of Heaven, Grimms' Tales for Young and Old*, translated by Ralph Manheim, Anchor Books, New York, 1977, was never far away. I was especially captured by one of Manheim's renderings, "Darling Roland." The fourth edition of *Roget's International Thesaurus*, revised by Robert L. Chapman, Thomas Y. Crowell Company, New York, 1977, was also at my side. I also found inspiration in *African-American Gardens and Yards in the Rural South* by Richard West Macott, the University of Tennessee Press, Knoxville, 1992. To the authors of these books, I am grateful.

CHAPTER ONE

It was the last day of school and the day before my thirteenth birthday. The temperature that afternoon had hit one hundred. After dinner, in our one-room apartment, it felt like one hundred and ten. I sat perched on the side of my bed near the fire-escape window, trying to catch some air. Sweat collected along the edges of my scalp, crisscrossing my face and dripping into my eyes. My big brother, Otis, lay sprawled on the red pullout couch with his mouth hanging open. Ma, already in her pajamas, sat motionless at the table in the center of the room, staring at the bills. I could hear kids' laughter and the cracking sound of a stick whacking a ball in the street below. In the projects across the way, a boom box pumped out a bass beat with too much reverb and a barrage of words sharp as bullets. Wailing in the distance was a siren. The world was going about its business in spite of the heat. But Ma had kept us in. Ma believed that the city wasn't safe for a girl in the evening. Otis she usually let roam. But tonight Otis was cooped up inside, too, on account of his report card. I glanced at my brother's face. He glared at me.

"What are you looking at?"

I lowered my eyes. "Nothing." It would be just like my brother to get three D's and an F, and then try to take it out on me.

"You'd better not be looking at me," he grumbled. "You scrawny little roach."

"You've got the face of a roach," I said, not skipping a beat. We enjoyed insulting each other.

Otis smirked and rubbed his chin. "Well, if you ask me, your growth is stunted."

"So is your brain."

He stretched his legs. "You've been reading too many books," he said. "You're beginning to smell like a worm."

"That's ridiculous," I snorted. "Worms don't even have a smell."

"Look at this six-pack," he bragged, baring his stomach. "I'm made of iron! Go ahead, hit me!"

I rolled my eyes. "You're pathetic."

He shot up from the couch. "Midget!"

"*Mental* midget!" I shot up from the bed.

"You think you're such a smart-ass!"

"At least I don't eat my toenails!" I zinged him.

The hint of a smile curled at the edges of his mouth. He towered over me. "You do pick your nose."

"That's a lie!"

"You're so short, I could cook potatoes and eat them off your wimpy little head!" he said, flicking me on the forehead.

"Oh yeah?" I jumped back. "Well, you couldn't cook a potato if you tried. Know why? Because you couldn't read the cookbook!" I got up in his face. "*Dumb*bell!"

Otis's brown eyes bugged out. I'd hit a nerve. He pulled a cushion off the couch and held it up threateningly.

"What are you going to do?" I taunted. "Smother me?"

He whacked me over the head!

"He hit me!" I cried.

I scrambled past the table where Ma was sitting. Otis tore after me. We zigzagged through the one-room apartment, running past the painted dresser and Ma's bed in the alcove. We circled the bathtub, which stood on four legs, and skidded by the sink filled with dishes. Then, lurching past the red couch, I lunged toward the fire escape. Otis grabbed me by the hair. We were half angry, half laughing.

"Ouch!" I screamed.

"Take it back!" Otis said, yanking my ponytail.

"Take what back?" I said, digging my fingernails into his hands.

"You called me a dummy!" he said, tightening his grip.

"I called you a dumb*bell*!" I screeched. "Not a dummy! Anyway, it's not my fault that you got a bad report card!" He pulled my hair even harder and I let out a bloodcurdling scream.

"That hurts! I'm not playing!"

From the center of the room, Ma's voice came thundering. "LET HER GO, OTIS MOON!" Otis let go and I dropped to my knees. We glanced at each other and then at Ma. I'd never heard her yell that loud in my life.

"I can't hear myself think!" Ma barked. "That scream almost split my eardrums!"

"It's not my fault," I whimpered, rubbing the back of my head where my hair had been pulled. "Otis was trying to scalp me. Degenerate fool!" I muttered under my breath.

Ma slammed her fist on the table. "That's enough, Mahalia!"

"Yes, Ma," I said obediently.

"And get up off the floor," she ordered. "I didn't pay an arm and a leg for those jeans you're wearing in order for you to tear them up roughhousing."

Otis gave me a hand and I clambered up onto my knees.

"We're sorry, Ma," he said nervously. "Please don't snap out on us."

"Snap out on *you?*" she shot back. "You two behave like three-year-olds!" She stood up. My mother is short, like I am. "You listen here, Otis. Your sister is right. You are a degenerate. Because only a degenerate would disappoint his mother the way you did with that lousy report card. Three D's and an F! Only a degenerate would say he's going to get a job to help out around here and then spend all his *durn* nights playing basketball across the street in that *durn* playground in the project!"

Otis and I stole a look at each other. Ma really hated cussing. Using the word *durn* was a big deal for our mother.

"See this mess!" She pointed to the jumble of bills. "I have to take care of this, nobody else. Your father isn't around asking about the rent increase, or the camp that Mahalia can't go to because we don't have the money, or the trip we want to make to Disney World! Or those size-twelve sneakers we couldn't afford, either, but just *had* to buy for you, Otis. Instead of helping me out, all you two can do is…disturb the *durn* peace!" She scrunched her face up like she was going to cry. She was so bent out of shape, she'd even mentioned Dad, whom we hadn't seen in years and never talked about.

"We didn't mean to upset you, Ma," I ventured timidly. "We didn't mean to disturb the durn peace."

"Nobody ever means anything!" she sobbed, collapsing at the table. "My boss at the hospital didn't mean it when she promised me the day off and then went back on her word! The landlord didn't mean it when he forgot for the umpteenth time to fix that cracked ceiling that any day is going to fall down and kill us! The president of the United States doesn't mean it, either!" She threw up her hands. "Give me a break, Lord!"

I stood there dumbfounded.

"Give *us* a break, Ma," my brother dared grumble. He slinked across the room and slammed his body down onto the couch, making the springs screech. "This is the last day of school," declared Otis. "We don't need no cryin' jag."

"And I don't need your disrespect," Ma countered, wiping her tears. "Nor do I need you to break the couch. So, if you don't mind, please don't throw yourself down on it next time. Please sit down on it properly. And while you're at it, you can locate the cushion that you hit your sister on the head with," she added, catching her breath.

"It's my couch," Otis muttered defiantly. "I'll do what I want with it. I'm the one who sleeps on it."

Ma's eyes watered. Otis was definitely taking advantage.

"Here's the cushion," I volunteered quickly. I picked it up, scurried across the room, and put it back into place. Ma had decided to ignore Otis's last remark. She blew her nose on a napkin.

"Someone could do the dinner dishes," she said with a little sniff.

Otis and I pointed at each other.

"Your turn!"

Ma's head dropped. "See what I mean?"

"Otis and I apologize, Ma," I said. I went up and patted her shoulder. "It's the last day of school. We're restless."

"It's hot as hell in this place, too," Otis complained. Ma gave him the evil eye.

"Hot as Hades," he corrected himself.

"I know," Ma muttered, wiping her brow. "I know you're hot, I know you're restless. I know it's the last day of school." She looked confused for an instant. "I can't solve all the world's problems. I'm only one person."

"We don't expect you to solve everything, Ma," I said gently.

Her face brightened for a minute. "Tell you one thing. I'm proud of that report card, Haley. All A's."

"Thanks," I said, flushing with pleasure.

"Grades ain't everything," Otis growled.

"Education is everything," Ma insisted.

"Oh yeah?" Otis cocked his head. "You got an education. How come you're just an admitting clerk at some hospital? You're probably smarter than a lot of them doctors."

"I went to night school," Ma objected. "I never got a degree. I hate to see you throw away your chances."

He shrugged. "What more can I do?"

"Apply yourself to your schoolwork," she snapped, "and stop picking on your sister. I can't stand all that bickering."

"Haley's the one who started it," Otis protested. "You were right here, Ma. You heard her."

Ma stared blankly. "I didn't hear anything."

"There wasn't anything to hear," I jumped in. "Otis just started picking on me."

"What was the fight about?" Ma asked.

Otis scratched his head. "Heck if I know. But I know that Haley started it."

"I didn't start it! You did!"

"You called me a dumb-ass," Otis declared.

"You called *me* a smart-ass," I argued. "A dumb*bell* is what I called you."

"Same thing," Otis said angrily. "You're putting me down because of the bad luck I had with my report card, and it wasn't even my fault."

"Whose fault was it?" I exclaimed.

"I have one of those learning disabilities," Otis said, pacing the room. He knocked his head with his fist. "That's the reason!"

"The only disability you have is that you don't study," I grumbled. "Anyway, you started the fight, because you knew I brought home a good report card and you got jealous!"

"You're always trying to show me up," Otis shouted.

"Shut up, you two!" Ma cried. There was a ragged edge to her voice, almost as if she were in pain. Otis and I got quiet.

"Are you okay, Ma?" I ventured.

She sighed. "Why don't we all have a glass of ice water?" she suggested. That was Ma's remedy for everything.

"I'll get it," volunteered Otis. He yanked open our tiny refrigerator. There was plenty of ice, but not much food. Otis cracked a tray of ice and divided it among three plastic tumblers. In a minute or two, we each had a tall drink in our hands.

"Thanks, Otis," Ma said, rubbing the tumbler along her forehead. A dark curl fell over one eye. She took a sip of water. "Ah, that's better."

Otis and I paused to drink our own water. A tiny breeze ventured in from the fire escape and slipped toward us. For a blessed instant, it was cool and quiet and nobody was getting on anyone's nerves. But then Otis made an announcement.

"I'm going out."

"You're grounded," Ma reminded him wearily. There were circles beneath her eyes.

"Are you okay, Ma?" I repeated.

"Fine," she replied. "Do the dishes."

I turned to the sink and ran the hot water. The steam hit me in the face, making me sweat again.

"You can't keep me cooped up in here," Otis said, slamming his glass down on the table. "It's the last day of school. Everybody in the world is outside but us. What is this? Some kind of prison?"

"Go ahead, Otis—insult the home I work hard to provide for you," countered Ma.

"I ain't insultin' nobody," Otis declared. "Just that I got to get out of this trap. Y'all two women be raggin' me night and day. You forgettin' that I'm the man around here! What yo' problem, Ma?" He strutted across the room. Otis loved the sound of his voice when he was talking that way. But it was just that tone of voice that always irritated Ma. And today it more than irritated her.

"My problem is that I have a fifteen-year-old son whose great ambition in life is to sound like a hoodlum," she said in a spurt. Then she started to cry again. Otis stared in surprise.

"He's sorry, Ma," I said, hurrying over.

"Yeah, I'm sorry," said Otis. "I'll do better in school next year. I promise. Besides, the reason I've got to go out tonight is to see about a job. I have one all lined up. I'm getting a job, Ma," he pressed, standing over her. "Isn't that what you want?"

"What kind of job?" I chimed in eagerly. "A job like Dill McCoy's?" Dill McCoy was the boyfriend of my next-door neighbor and former baby-sitter, Nirvana Brown.

Otis scowled. "No, definitely not a job like Dill McCoy's. I ain't going to spend my summer being some low-paid burger flipper."

"What are you going to do, then?" I persisted. "Work at the sneaker store, like Nirvana does?"

"Why is everybody always throwing those two up in my face?" Otis scoffed. "There are other people in the world with jobs besides Nirvana Brown and Dill McCoy."

"What kind of job do you have in mind, Otis?" Ma asked quietly.

He rubbed his chin. "I'm going into business for myself."

"An entrepreneur!" I exclaimed.

He frowned. "What's that?"

"A person who goes into business for himself," I said, scrubbing a plate. "I learned the word in school."

"*Entrepreneur.*" Otis rolled the word around in his mouth. "You got that right, Sis," he said, crossing the room. "And tonight is the night I'm getting my entrepreneur situation all set up." He pushed open the front door and left.

"How come he gets to go out?" I complained, flicking the suds off my fingers. "You said he was grounded."

"I can't control him," Ma admitted. "Besides, he's seeing about a job." She gathered up the bills and buried them beneath the knives in the silverware drawer.

"Aren't those the bills?" I asked with a worried glance.

"Yes. I've paid what I can. They'll just have to wait for the rest," she said, slamming the drawer.

"Is that okay?"

She kissed me on the cheek. "Don't worry so much, Mahalia."

"So, can I go out tonight, too?" I asked, rinsing a glass.

"No way," Ma said, grabbing a dish towel.

"How is that fair?" I sulked. "Otis got all D's and an F. I got all A's."

"Where would you go?" Ma asked.

"To a movie or something."

"With whom?"

"With myself. I can't go with my friend Gina. She's packing for camp. She leaves in the morning."

Ma picked up a plate and wiped it. "Sorry," she said with a sigh. "You're not going out by yourself in New York City with no place to go and nobody to go with at nine o'clock at night."

She gave me another kiss on the cheek. "You'll grow up soon enough. Then you'll have all the freedom you want. You'll travel all over the world, I bet."

She placed the dish towel on the counter and crossed to her alcove. She tossed me a little smile. "What kind of birthday cake do you want tomorrow?"

"Same as always, chocolate." I grinned. "Some things never change, I guess."

"But some things do," Ma said wistfully. "I can't believe my baby is turning thirteen."

She climbed into bed, pulled the sheet up to her chin, and closed her eyes. I stood there.

What had happened to the ma who used to stay up later than I did? The one who, only a few months ago, insisted on tucking me in? The one who rarely yelled and never cried? She was definitely upset about something. But what? Nothing unusual had happened. Maybe she was sad about Grandma Dora, it occurred to me. When Grandma Dora had died, Ma had cried an awful lot. But that was five whole years ago. *Maybe there are some things you never get over,* I thought, turning around to let out the dishwater.

There was a tiny window above the sink. Perched on the sill was our cookie jar. We'd had it for as long as I could remember—a clown cookie jar, wearing a yellow clown's hat and a yellow suit with bright red buttons. I remembered Grandma Dora filling it up with oatmeal cookies. Of course, the cookie jar hadn't always been cracked like it was now, I reminded myself. My finger rested on the gash between the clown's two top buttons. That had been Dad's doing.... My only other clear memory of my grandmother was of her singing a hymn about walking alone in a garden with some dew on some roses.

I dried my hands and listened for Ma's snoring. The room was quiet, which meant she wasn't asleep yet, but only pretending to be. She was lying so still it was almost as if she were pretending to be a corpse. I crept over to my own bed and looked out the fire-escape window. Across the street, the playground lights had come on. I sat down on my bed and lowered my hand into the cardboard box where I kept my special things, like my stuffed snake and Grandma Dora's pearl earrings. It's where I also kept a book I owned, a collection of Grimms' fairy tales. The Grimm brothers wrote the stories in German. My book was an English translation with brightly colored illustrations. Ma and Dad had given Grimms' to me a long, long time ago. I picked up the book and stroked the painting on the cover. It was a picture of Hansel and Gretel walking through a dense forest along a path of gleaming silver pebbles. That was from the part in the story where the path of pebbles that Hansel had made showed him and his sister the way home. Of course, when their father left them in the forest, he hadn't planned on them coming home at all. The plan was that the two kids would die. But they hadn't! I knew that it was utterly stupid for a girl my age to be reading fairy tales, but I liked my *Grimms'*.

One of my very favorite stories was called "Darling Roland." The girl in the story turned herself into things. First she turned herself into a duck, which was kind of ridiculous, then into a red stone, then later on into a flower. But the very beginning was so gruesome. The girl's wicked stepmother committed a murder. When the girl woke up, she was lying next to a severed head. She tucked the head under her arm, and drops of blood fell onto the floor. The drops of blood had voices. Then the girl ran away with a guy named Darling Roland.

I smiled and put the book down next to my pillow, then went out to the bathroom in the hall. There was only a john and a sink in the hallway bathroom. We shared it with Nirvana and her grandmother. They had their own bathtub in their apartment, just like we did.

When I came back inside, Ma was snoring, which meant she was sleeping for real. I put on my yellow pajamas that crept up to my shins, knelt down on the floor, and said my prayers.

God bless Ma and Otis. And God bless Dad, wherever he is.

God bless Grandma Dora up in heaven. Thank you for my report card, and please let me get a summer job. And even though we need the rain, don't let it rain on my birthday. Amen.

I fell asleep reading my book.

CHAPTER TWO

Next morning, the sun woke me up, along with two voices screeching in my ears. Ma and Otis were singing to me.

"Happy birthday to you, happy birthday to YOU!" My eyes shot open and Ma and Otis both started tickling me at the same time.

"Quit it!" I choked, rolling up into a ball. Ma was after my stomach, while Otis tickled the back of my neck. "Quit it!" I howled. "You're going to make me wet the bed!" Otis backed off, holding his nose.

"Eeew! A thirteen-year-old bed wetter!"

"I didn't say that I *had* wet the bed," I grumbled, tossing my legs over the side. The sun through the window was bright. I was already sweating. But I was glad that it wasn't raining. "I said I *would* wet the bed if you didn't stop tickling me."

"Go to the john then, sweetie," Ma said. Her brown eyes sparkled. I hadn't seen her look so happy in a while. "We just wanted to wake you up with a big 'happy birthday,' " she said.

"Thanks," I said, grinning sheepishly. I hobbled toward the door. "But first things first."

Fortunately, the bathroom was empty. It smelled of ammonia, as it did every morning. The lucky thing about sharing the john with Nirvana and Mrs. Brown was that Mrs. Brown loved to clean. Even the bar of soap on the ledge next to the sink looked brand-new today. That business done, I scooted back into the apartment and immediately tripped on something. I spied a grapefruit lying at my feet. "What's a grapefruit doing on the floor?" I yelped.

Otis hooted. "Ask Ma."

I blinked and cast my eyes around. Otis was perched on the windowsill next to my bed, and Ma stood at the stove, smiling. Everywhere else I looked there were grocery bags. "Where did all this come from?" I had never seen so much food before!

"I bought it," said Ma.

I wandered around the room. There were eggplants in the bathtub, along with three jars of peanut butter. I rubbed my eyes. "Was this here when I went to the bathroom?"

Otis nodded. "Guess you had to go so bad you didn't notice."

I glanced at Ma again. "But where did it come from?"

"The all-night grocery store. A dream woke me up at two A.M. So I decided to go shopping."

Otis rolled his eyes. "I came home just in time to help her carry the stuff upstairs. Ma thinks that the world is going to end," he joked.

I counted the bags. There were twenty. "All this must have cost a lot," I muttered.

"I charged it," Ma explained. "I needed to do the shopping for your birthday dinner. While I was at it, I got a few other things."

"What are we having to eat for my birthday dinner?" I asked, perking up.

Otis wrinkled his nose. "Duck with oranges."

"Duck à l'orange," she corrected him.

"Sounds fancy," I said. "Is the duck in one of these?" I asked, peeking into the bags.

"In here," Ma said. She opened the refrigerator and a spiny green thing fell out.

"What's that?" I asked, jumping back.

"Artichoke." She picked up the green thing and stuffed it back in, then pulled out a carton of eggs. "You'll see the duck later," she said. "What about a twelve-egg omelet for breakfast?"

I laughed. "Maybe I should have an omelet with two eggs so that I can save room for my dinner."

"What is duck with oranges, anyway?" Otis asked.

"A yummy French dish," Ma said, cracking some eggs into a bowl. "I had it with my co-worker Sylvia when we took her out to celebrate before she got married. It came to me in the middle of the night in that dream."

"You dreamed about ducks, Ma?" I asked, setting the table.

She nodded. "They were flying around with orange balloons in their mouths. That's what made me think of cooking the dish. I hurried right out to get the ingredients. Nothing's too good for my daughter on her thirteenth birthday!"

"What about me?" Otis bristled. "I got the job I was after. It's all set up. Nobody's saying anything about that."

"You got the job?" I exclaimed. "That's great! What kind of job is it?"

"Working with a guy at an incense stand," he reported.

"I thought you said you were going into business for yourself," I reminded him.

"I am, sort of," he hedged. "Me and my friend are going into business together. Actually, my friend started it."

"Isn't that nice?" Ma said, smiling while she cooked.

"You're going to be selling incense?" I asked.

Otis grinned. "This friend of mine said that you make *boo-koo* money at those stands."

I went over and slapped him five. "Congratulations!"

"Thanks, Haley!"

"Very industrious," Ma commented, scooping some scrambled eggs onto two plates.

"I thought you were making omelets," I reminded her.

"Did I say that?" she remarked. "I don't know which is more scrambled, these eggs or my brains." She set the plates down with a nervous laugh. "Come and get it, you two."

Otis clambered over to the table and I took a seat. "These are delicious, Ma," I said, digging in.

"I'd pour you some orange juice," she murmured distractedly, "but I'm afraid if I open the refrigerator again, something else will fall out."

"Why don't you have some breakfast yourself?" Otis suggested. "You always say that breakfast is the most important meal of the day."

"I'll get something later," Ma muttered, crossing to her alcove. "First I want to give Haley her presents."

I drew in a breath. "Did I hear the word *presents?*" I squeaked.

"They're from Ma," said Otis. "I haven't gotten you anything yet, but I have something planned."

"Here we are," Ma said. She reached under her bed and pulled out two wrapped packages, a big one and a little one. I pushed my plate aside, and she set the boxes in front of me. The bows on the gifts were gold and the paper was lavender.

"Oh, Ma!" I gasped. "Those are beautiful!" I stared at the gifts. "I've never seen such pretty wrapping before."

"I had it done at the store," Ma said.

"Rip them open!" Otis demanded.

"Hold your horses," I said, reaching for the bigger box and gently tugging on one of the gold bows. "I want to save the paper if I can."

Ma stroked my head. "Good girl, Haley."

I carefully loosened the lavender paper from around a box with pink stripes. I took off the top and reached in. Nestled in folds of tissue paper was something soft and deliciously smooth. "What is it?" I whispered.

"Take it out!" Otis said impatiently.

I pulled out a blue jacket and matching long, flowing

pants. "Gorgeous!" I breathed. I had never owned anything so lovely.

"They're pajamas," said Ma.

"Boring," said Otis.

"They are not boring!" I said, stroking the sleeve of the jacket. "I love them!" Ma's eyes watered.

"Glad you like them, baby. They're silk."

"Silk pajamas, wow!" I hugged the outfit close.

"It's kind of a practical gift," Ma said apologetically, "but still kind of special."

"Better than those funky yellow pajamas she's been wearing for the past three years," quipped Otis.

"They're such a nice blue," I murmured, trying to ignore him.

"Better open the other one before I do," Otis teased, grabbing the smaller box. I snatched the gift out of his hand, this time undoing the paper more quickly. The gift was a paperback book that reminded me of a dictionary.

"A thesaurus," I announced, reading the title.

"I thought it would come in handy," explained Ma. "You can look up a word and find lots of other words that mean the same thing."

"Wow!" I said, leafing through the book. I had never

seen so many words! "What's another word for *beauty?*" I quizzed Otis.

"I don't want to know," he said, putting his hands over his ears.

I stood up and yelled in his face. "*Pulchritude!* My new pajamas are very pulchritudinous!" Otis put down his hands and screwed up his face.

"For you, I'll look up all the words for *ugly!*" I teased.

"Tell her to stop, Ma!" Otis complained. "She's going to use that book to insult me. The other day she called me a roach!"

"I should have called you a *rogue,*" I said with a giggle. "It means a person who's mischievous."

"Can't call me any names now that I have a job," Otis insisted, crossing his arms on his chest.

"Not even an entrepreneur?" I prodded.

"Well, maybe that one," he said.

I turned to Ma and gave her a hug. "Thanks for the presents. They're great."

"You're welcome," Ma said, hugging me back tightly.

"Thanks, Otis," I added.

"Told you I had nothing to do with that stuff," he reminded me. "I would have gotten you something more exciting, like a basketball. See you later. I've got to go to work."

"Good luck," I said, grabbing his waist.

"Let go of me, girl!" he said, yanking away. "You've got cooties!"

"And you've got athlete's foot between your eyes," I zinged him.

"Don't start," Ma warned, pushing us apart. She stood on her toes and gave Otis a kiss on the cheek. "Be back early for Haley's birthday dinner."

He hopped out the door. "Don't burn it, Ma!" he called with a hoot.

"What a thing to say," Ma mumbled. She glanced around. "I certainly bought enough food, didn't I?"

"We can eat lots of vegetables with the duck," I suggested, dashing into the corner to try on my pajamas.

Turning her back to give me privacy, Ma crossed to the stove. "Good idea, Haley. I have a butternut squash that I'm dying to bake."

I slipped on the pants and then the jacket. They felt so smooth next to my skin. I waltzed out into the room. "What do you think?" I asked, making a pirouette.

Ma watched admiringly. "Nice. A perfect fit."

"Can I wear them during the day?" I asked eagerly.

She chuckled and picked up the coffeepot.

"Not even out on the fire escape?" I asked, dashing for the window next to my bed. I scooted up onto the sill before Ma could stop me.

"Where are you going in your nightclothes, Mahalia Moon?" she called, following me with the pot in her hand.

"Out!" I cried, climbing out the window and onto the fire escape.

Ma stuck her head out. "Come back here!"

"Relax, Ma. Nobody's watching."

"There are people on the street," she insisted.

"Then come and get me," I teased. Ma took a step back. Her hair was wrapped up in an old scarf. I knew that my mother would drop dead before she stepped onto anybody's fire escape looking like that.

"Come in here, Haley," she called helplessly.

I looked up. My new blue pajamas matched the sky! I spread my arms out. What a perfect day! Another scorcher, maybe, but a scorcher with a beautiful breeze. Sunlight bounced off the red brick of the buildings. Even the cars on the street seemed to gleam. And down below on our stoop, Nirvana and Dill sat kissing. Next year, they would be seniors, and they planned to get married when they graduated.

"Hey, Nirvana!" I yelled. She looked up. Her gold earrings gave off a glint. Her head was a sculpture of braids.

"Happy birthday, Haley!" She'd remembered!

Dill waved. He was wearing his restaurant uniform. Ma's hospital gave her Saturdays off, but Dill and Nirvana usually worked on weekends.

"Hey, little chick!" Dill called up. "What are you going to do on your birthday?"

"Eat duck with oranges!" I shouted.

"Come in with those nightclothes on," Ma scolded, pushing half her body out the window. She had taken off the scarf and combed her hair. "Come in!" she insisted, grabbing my hand.

"Okay, okay," I said, relenting. She stepped aside so that I could climb in. "What makes you think they have to be nightclothes?" I asked. "If I'm wearing them now, aren't they *day*clothes?"

"Don't give me lip," Ma said, wagging her finger.

I smiled and grabbed my jeans off a chair. "Just teasing, Ma. I'll get dressed."

"Go out and have fun," she encouraged, turning to the stove. "Coffee should be done soon. Want some?"

"No thanks," I said, pulling on my top. I folded the new pajamas and made up my bed. Then I grabbed my thesaurus.

"Where are you off to?" she asked.

"Nowhere special," I replied. "Maybe the park. Maybe I'll go to the grocery store and look at the bulletin board. I might find a baby-sitting job."

Ma stared off into space.

"Want to come?" I asked her.

"I've got a lot of preparation to do," she said, snapping out of it. "I've got to whip things into shape."

"Want me to help?"

"You go," Ma prodded. "It's your birthday." She hurried across the room to the dresser. In the top drawer, there was a pay envelope. "Buy yourself a doughnut," she said, handing me five dollars.

I gave her a kiss. "Thanks, Ma," I breathed. "That will buy more than one doughnut, though. I'll put the rest away."

She pinched my cheek. "You look taller today."

"You think so?" I asked eagerly.

She nodded. "You grew in your sleep."

I strode to the door and looked over my shoulder. Eggplants were still in the bathtub, and bags were strewn everywhere. A knot tightened in my stomach. "Don't work too hard, Ma!"

"Don't worry about me!" she called, suddenly whizzing about. She dumped a bag of vegetables out on the table, reached for a box of sugar from the cabinet, tugged open a drawer, and pulled out a knife. Then she yanked open the refrigerator and an orange rolled out.

"I'll pull this party together in ten seconds flat!" Ma said, tossing me a huge smile. She poured herself some coffee. I waved and banged the door shut.

I headed straight for Rivera's. Mr. Rivera himself sold me a coconut-cream chocolate doughnut. I sank my teeth in, right then and there at the counter. "These are the best!" I exclaimed, licking a drop of cream filling off the side of my finger. Mr. Rivera nodded appreciatively. He had a streak of flour in his gray hair and a jelly stain on his white apron.

"You seem cheerful," he commented.

"It's my birthday," I announced, pushing my way out through the jingling door. I popped the rest of the doughnut into my mouth, swallowing its sweetness, and crossed the street. A morsel of coconut remained on my tongue, and I mashed it onto the roof of my mouth. Finding a free bench in the park, I sat down to watch. There were so many people in the park! People with dogs, and women in sunglasses. Girls wearing hoop earrings, men who looked rich and fashionable, men who looked all worn out. Two boys on skateboards, carrying boom boxes, and a little girl in a stroller hanging on to a balloon. In the middle of the grass, a lady slept on a blanket next to a shopping cart, and on a bench nearby, a man in cowboy boots read a newspaper. The sun sparkled over all of them.

I opened my thesaurus and looked up words. Another word for hot was *torrid*. Something sweet could be called *mellifluous*. Something fragrant might be *odoriferous*. *Charm* could also mean *magnetism*. There was a whole string of words that meant *stench: stink, fetidness, foulness, funkiness*....I looked up and a big boy with a leer in his eye was heading right toward me.

"Let me see your fine booty, baby!" he called menacingly.

I jumped up. "GET LOST, FUNKY FOULNESS!" I screamed in his face. Then I ran as fast as I could. Stuff like that scared me, but Otis had taught me to act fast and tough.

Out of sight of the boy in the park, I scooted into the grocery store. After catching my breath, I looked at the bulletin board. There were no notices for baby-sitting, but there was an ad that looked interesting.

YARD HELPER WANTED. STRONG WORKER NEEDED TO CLEAN UP YARD FOR NEIGHBORHOOD SINGING TEACHER. GOOD PAY. START IMMEDIATELY. On the bottom of the notice there were little tabs listing an address not far away. I tore off one of the tabs. I hadn't seen many yards in New York, unless you counted the community garden, which was pretty nice. Ma had taken us on the subway to the Brooklyn Botanic Garden. It was exquisite. I'll never forget the dazzling red tulips. The pink azaleas there were so bright that you saw spots in front of your eyes if you stared at them for too long.

Ducking out of the store, I took off for the address, which was only a few blocks away. I found the house easily. It was a tall and narrow dark brick building. One of those old-fashioned-looking houses that hadn't been divided up into apartments yet. On the front of the house were two tall windows with flowing white curtains inside and curvy black iron grilles outside. The front steps were made of gray stone. Altogether, the house looked very fancy. I stood on the sidewalk admiring it. I figured that the yard was in the back, since I didn't see one out front.

I ventured up the steps to the polished wooden door. Just as I was about to ring the doorbell, I heard music. Someone was playing the piano! Piano was my favorite instrument. We had one in our chorus room at school. I sat down on the steps to listen. Whoever was playing had really fast fingers. Notes were flying everywhere! The music cascaded out the windows: high notes and low notes and chords that came crashing. I closed my eyes and drew in a breath. It was like a sparkling waterfall, tumbling into a river and taking me with it. Tears came to my eyes. Any moment I thought that someone would begin singing something from a grand opera. But the piano went on alone, startling the air and then wrapping itself around me. Then, abruptly, the music stopped. I went up and rang the bell. A tall, striking man opened the door. His face was elegant, but he was wearing a T-shirt. I glanced at his hands, which were huge, then up at his eyes, which were jet-black with thick, curling lashes.

He smiled. "May I help you?"

"I came about the yard job," I said with a swallow. I looked at him in awe. "Was that you playing the piano?"

He nodded. "I made a few mistakes, I'm afraid."

"I thought it was incredible!" I said eagerly. "I was sitting here listening. I hope that was okay."

He laughed. "Thanks. Come again anytime. I'm not a professional piano player, but I could always use an appreciative audience."

"So, are you the singing teacher in the ad?" I asked. I held out the paper with the address.

"The same," he replied. "My name is D'Angola Jackson."

"My name is Mahalia Moon. Is the yard helper job still open?"

"This is a job for a hulk," he said apologetically. "There's a lot of heavy lifting."

"I'm pretty strong," I volunteered.

He looked at his watch. "Can you come back later? I'm expecting a slew of students, and one any minute. Can you come back at six o' clock?"

"I'm not sure," I replied hesitantly. "My mother is making a dinner."

Just then a slim young woman in a red-flowered dress

walked up. She had something tucked under her arm that looked like sheet music.

"Hi, Shari," he said.

She smiled. "Hi, Jackson."

Jackson stepped aside and she walked in.

"Try to come back," he said, giving me a little wave. "If not tonight, then tomorrow."

I stuffed the slip of paper into my pocket and Mr. Jackson shut the door. He'd said that he wanted a hulk for the job, but maybe I had a chance. Otherwise, why would he have asked me to come back? If I couldn't come back at six, I promised myself, I would definitely come back tomorrow. I started for home. Maybe I could help Ma make the birthday cake.

I could never have imagined what I found back at home. First of all, there was smoke in the hallway. I ran up the stairs. Our apartment door was open. Otis stood in the doorway, and I could see Nirvana just inside. I heard someone crying.

"Ma burned your birthday cake," Otis announced as I rushed past the two of them. Nirvana's grandmother, Mrs. Brown, was standing next to the table. Ma was sitting at the table, wringing her hands and sobbing. She was surrounded by all kinds of vegetables, some peeled and cut up, some already cooked, and others still wrapped in plastic. In the middle of it all, still in its pan, was a smoldering cake.

"Don't cry, Ma," I said, hugging her. "We can bake another one."

She laid down her head and kept sobbing.

"Your mother has been this way for two hours," Mrs. Brown informed me. "I heard her crying and knocked on the door." She clucked her tongue. "She's broke down."

Fear clutched at my chest. "Stop crying, Ma," I said, patting her on the back. "We can buy a birthday cake at the store." She sobbed louder still.

"Stop crying, Ma!" Otis demanded.

Ma lifted her head for a moment. "I'm sorry, kids," she managed to get out. "I have to go to the hospital."

My mouth went dry. "You're going to work?"

"Not to work," she said, catching her breath. "I have to get help."

"She needs a doctor!" Mrs. Brown's voice clanged over the din.

Suddenly, Nirvana was next to me. "Don't worry,

Haley," she said softly. "We'll take care of you while your mother's gone."

"She ain't going nowhere!" Otis said angrily.

I clutched Ma's hand. She looked at me helplessly. "See that?" she asked, pointing to one of the vegetables. It was a cooked butternut squash, split open in a baking pan. A jumble of white seeds lay nestled in the heart of its dark orange flesh.

"You see that?" said Ma, her voice rising. "That's me, Haley!"

I blinked. "No, it's not."

"That's me," she insisted.

Otis put his hands over his ears. "Shut up!"

"I can't work things out anymore," Ma said, struggling to speak through her tears. "I feel like the jumble of seeds in that squash." She looked away. "Forgive me, Haley. It'll just be for a little while."

"Things will be okay," Mrs. Brown said, helping Ma up.

They walked across to the closet and got out the suitcase.

"How long will you be gone?" I cried, following her.

"It won't be long," Mrs. Brown said, answering for Ma.

"Ma?" I clung to her elbow as she reached for her clothes. "You can't just leave us like this!"

Her face crumpled. "Try to be patient, darling."

She crossed to the dresser, opened the top drawer, and took out her pay envelope. She pressed what was left in it, a twenty-dollar bill, into Mrs. Brown's hand. "Use this if they need something," she said. "There are plenty of groceries."

Mrs. Brown took the money and nodded.

"Why are you so sad, Ma?" I asked, crowding up close. Otis stood slouching near by.

"Snap out of it, Ma," he begged. "It's just a stupid birthday cake. It's just a stupid squash."

"Do you miss Grandma Dora, Ma?" I whimpered. "Is that why you're crying?"

Ma squeezed her eyes shut. "I have to do this," she whispered fiercely. "Otis, take care of your sister. Now, leave me alone...."

CHAPTER THREE

I lay scrunched up on my bed, waiting for the phone to ring. It was another stifling night. A fly had gotten in and was buzzing around the ceiling near the light. Ma had said that she'd call us, but she hadn't. Nirvana had offered to sleep over in the apartment with us, but Otis had said no way. Then Mrs. Brown had asked me if I wanted to sleep over with them. I couldn't, because of her cats. She seemed to have forgotten that I was allergic to them. After all that had happened, I had no desire to itch and wheeze all night long and turn into one giant pimple. So it was just Otis and me.

The first thing my brother did after the Browns left was to go out and buy ice cream. Oddly enough, ice cream was the one thing Ma seemed to have forgotten to buy. Maybe she had had a premonition about the doomed cake. Along with the ice cream, my brother also brought back a tiny television!

"Where'd you get that?" I asked in amazement. Our own television had been broken for ages; Ma had stored it in the back of the closet.

"I borrowed it from a friend of mine," Otis said, setting it on the floor. He plugged it in while I dished out the ice cream. Then the two of us camped out in front of it.

"What's your friend's name?" I asked.

"Reggie," he replied. "He's the one with the incense stand." Otis patted my knee. "I thought you might like it. Get your mind off things."

"Thanks, Otis," I said, scooting closer.

He turned to a nighttime talk show. Otis laughed at a guy telling jokes, but I couldn't make myself follow him. There was this sick feeling in the pit of my stomach. I picked at my ice cream. "Why isn't she calling us?"

"More than likely, it's too late," Otis said, keeping his eyes glued to the screen. "She'll call us in the morning."

"What do they do to people who cry too much?" I asked, touching his elbow.

"How should I know?" he responded. "They probably put Ma in the psych ward with all the other nutty people."

I hung my head. A tear rolled down my cheek. "She isn't a nut. She's our mother."

"Don't cry, Haley." He reached over and wiped away my tear. "But I do think that Ma is a little bit crazy. Didn't you notice how weird she was acting?"

"She seemed tired," I admitted. "She was zoning out. I hope she feels better now that she's at the hospital."

"People know Ma at the hospital," Otis reminded me. "They'll fix her up. Probably give her some kind of pills or something." He cocked his head. "I wonder if she admitted herself. She *is* one of the admitting clerks."

"Be serious, Otis," I objected.

"I know a brother whose mom had a breakdown," Otis reported. "She pulled through."

"A breakdown?" I said in a shaky voice. "Is that what you think happened to Ma?"

"We'll find out tomorrow," Otis said. "We can't do nothin' about it now." With a determined look on his face, he screwed his eyes back to the television.

I wandered over to my bed, my heart thudding. I curled up, hoping to hear the telephone. My thesaurus was next to my pillow, along with my *Grimms'*. I looked for the moon, but clouds had covered it. Then I noticed an edge of silver light, which I took for a crescent. I waited for the moon to appear, but it never did. Maybe that edge was all there was left of the moon, I thought, covering my head with a pillow. Maybe the moon had burned out.

*　　*　　*

The next morning, Otis woke me up with a basketball!

"Will you shut up?" I groaned, rolling over. Yucky drool was in the corner of my mouth.

"This is for you," he said, directing a hoop shot toward the trash can. "It's your birthday present."

"Why didn't you give it to me yesterday?" I asked, wiping my face with the back of my hand.

"I didn't have it yesterday," Otis said, looping the room. "My buddy gave it to me this morning, when I took back the television."

"Your buddy sure has a lot of stuff," I commented in a groggy voice.

Otis winked. "He knows what he's doing."

I sat up on my elbow and sighed. The place looked like it had been bombed. Vegetables and grocery bags were strewn everywhere. "Did Ma call while I was asleep?" I asked hopefully.

"Too early," said Otis. He threw the ball and I ducked. "Get you some breakfast before I get out of here."

"Speak good English," I snapped at him.

"I'll speak the way I want," Otis snapped back. "You're not my mother."

"And you're not my father!"

"Got that right," Otis muttered, picking the ball up off the floor.

"So, what do we do?" I asked, throwing my legs across the side of the bed.

"About what?"

"About Ma—what do you think? What's wrong with you, Otis?" I griped. "You act like nothing happened. This is serious."

"I know that," he said, leaning against the door. "That's why I'm taking care of business. The best way we can help Ma is to work hard and be strong."

"Sounds good," I admitted. "I just wish I knew how she's doing."

"Call the hospital," he said. "There's the phone."

I stared at the telephone. "But Ma said that she would call us."

"So what?" he said with a shrug. "Give it a try. Tell her we're worried about her."

"What number should I call?" I asked, crossing to the telephone.

"Call Ma's work number," Otis suggested. "Maybe Sylvia will be there and tell you how to get in touch with her."

"Maybe you should call," I said, getting cold feet. Suppose something really bad had happened?

"You're the one who can't wait to talk to Ma," Otis said stubbornly. "You do it."

I dialed Ma's work number. A familiar voice answered.

"Admitting. Sylvia Coleman speaking."

"Hi, Sylvia. It's Haley Moon."

There was a pause. I drew in a breath.

"How are you?" asked Sylvia.

"We're okay. I'm calling about my mother. Did you see her?"

"I peeked in on her this morning. I heard that she was upstairs when I came in today," said Sylvia. I glanced at Otis, who by this time was standing next to me.

"Is she okay?"

"She's in good hands," said Sylvia.

I breathed a sigh of relief.

"Someone in the office wangled her a private room," Sylvia said. "I'll look up the number."

"Ma has a telephone number of her own," I whispered to Otis. "Get something to write with."

Otis found a pen on the cluttered table and tore off a

piece of brown paper bag. When Sylvia came back on the line, I wrote down the number.

"Thanks, Sylvia."

"Are you kids okay over there? Is somebody with you?"

"We have our neighbor, Mrs. Brown," I replied. "Her daughter used to baby-sit me."

"Nice to have neighbors like that," said Sylvia. "I'll reassure your ma when I see her that you kids are doing just fine."

"I think I'll call Ma myself now," I said. "Thanks for everything, Sylvia."

I clicked down the phone.

"Feel better?" asked Otis.

I nodded. "Let's call her now," I said eagerly.

Otis lowered his eyes. "You go ahead. I don't want to talk to her."

"How come?"

"I just don't," Otis said firmly.

I tried Ma's number. The phone rang and rang. "Maybe she's still asleep," I said nervously. She answered just as I was about to give up.

"Hello?" Her voice was so soft that I hardly recognized it.

"Ma? It's me!" I heard a sniff on the other end of the line.

"You said that you were going to call us last night. I was worried," I went on.

"I was going to call you, precious," she said in a slightly stronger voice. "You and Otis doing all right?"

"We're fine," I assured her.

"Did you sleep at Mrs. Brown's?"

"I'm allergic to cats, Ma. Don't tell me you forgot, too?"

There was a long pause.

"What did the doctor say?" I jumped in. "When are you coming home?"

She sighed. "Could be a few weeks."

A wave of panic washed over me. A few weeks! I had figured she'd only be gone a couple of days. "Aren't there some pills you can take?"

"He has me on something," she said flatly. Then her voice rose. "Promise you'll listen to Mrs. Brown."

"Okay," I said. "Can we visit?"

She drew in a breath. "Yes. You're old enough."

"When are visiting hours?" I asked.

"Three o' clock, I think." She sighed. "Put your brother on."

I turned around to look for Otis. But he was gone.

"I—I can't find him," I stuttered. "I'm going to come and see you. Okay?"

She burst into tears. "I have to go, sweetheart. Be strong."

I was still holding the receiver when Otis walked back into the room.

"Where were you?" I asked. "She wanted to speak to you."

"In the bathroom," he said with a shrug. "How does she sound?"

I hung my head. "Still upset. She didn't even say good-bye to me. The doctor did give her some pills," I added hopefully. "We can go see her at three o' clock."

"Not me," said Otis. "I've got work to do."

"You're not going to visit Ma?" I was dumbfounded. "Suppose she wants to see you?"

"I don't care," Otis said, setting his jaw. "I don't want to see my mother acting stupid like that, crying over a stupid squash."

"I don't understand you, Otis," I complained.

"The best thing we can do for Ma is to clean this place up," he said, pointing to the mess in the apartment. "And I have to work. Who knows how much money she has in the bank?"

"She hid some of the bills," I said in a worried voice.

"See what I mean?" said Otis. "We got to let the doctor take care of Ma. We got to take care of us."

"You talk as if she's going to be there forever," I snapped.

"How long did she say it would be?" he asked.

"Maybe a few weeks," I sighed. "She's still crying like she was last night. But I'm going to visit her anyway."

"That's your business," said Otis, folding his arms across his chest. "She told us to leave her alone, remember?"

"She didn't mean that," I said with a sigh.

"You got to hold on to yourself, Haley," he said, jutting out his chin. "Know what I mean?"

I shrugged. "Not really, but that's okay. Maybe I can get Nirvana to go with me."

"Good idea," said Otis.

I stared at the burned cake on the counter. "Where should we start around here?"

"Toss that first," said Otis. "Why do we need a burned cake when there's enough food here to feed an army?"

I dumped the cake into the trash can. Spying the butternut squash in the sink, I ruthlessly scooped it up.

"This definitely goes out," I said grimly.

"Amen," said Otis.

We put all the vegetables that we could fit into the refrigerator and stacked up the rest in a corner. We lined the walls with the extra canned food.

"Now, breakfast," my brother ordered.

I shook my head. "I'm totally *un*hungry after putting all this food away."

"The sight of it makes me want to puke," he agreed. "Maybe Nirvana's grandmother could make you some eggs or something."

"I'm not starting the day with hives," I said, stalking across the room. I grabbed some fresh clothes out of the dresser.

"See you later, then," he said. "I've got to meet Reggie."

"Where's he live?" I asked.

"Across the street," Otis muttered. "Dill knows him. His apartment is on the same floor."

I smiled. "He must be nice if Dill knows him."

"Reggie doesn't hang with that loser Dill. Reggie has it together." He gave me a wink. "Hang tough, Haley. If Ma sees you acting like a wimp, it'll just make things worse for her."

"I'll do my best," I promised. My brother left. The eggplants were out of the tub, so I took a quick bath and then put on my clothes, overalls and a nice T-shirt. I thought of wearing my new blue pajama top beneath the overalls, but I knew that Ma wouldn't like that. "Hang tough," I repeated to myself, combing my hair in the mirror. I fastened it back with a big clip. I spied Ma's Cinnamon Doll lipstick and put some on. Now that I was thirteen, I figured that I could wear makeup. I wanted to look halfway decent when I went to visit Ma at the hospital. But before I did that, I had time to go see the singing teacher. More than ever, I wanted that yard job. Otis and I had enough food, but what about the bills, the ones Ma hadn't paid? I tucked my wallet into one of my pockets and stuck my thesaurus into the other one. After fishing my key out of the jeans I'd worn the day before, I walked out and locked the apartment behind me. An instant after I stepped into the hallway, the door to the Browns' place flew open.

"Where are you going?" Mrs. Brown asked, wedging forward slowly.

"I have to see about a job," I said, jamming the key into my pocket next to my wallet. "Then I have to see Ma."

"I thought that you and Otis would go to church with

me this morning," she said. She rested her weight on one leg and then on the other. "Nirvana is coming. She's just in the bathtub."

"I can't go today," I said. "And Otis is working."

Mrs. Brown raised an eyebrow. "On Sunday?"

"Yes, ma'am."

"Well, I'll do what I can for you kids," said Mrs. Brown. She smiled. She had the kind of smile that any minute could turn into a frown. "But you have to remember that my legs are bad, so I can't run around keeping up with you. The only time I go out is on Sunday to church, and then I take a cab. I raised my only child already, Haley," she added. "I have all I can handle with Nirvana."

She paused. "Did you speak with your mother yet?"

"This morning," I told her. "I was hoping that Nirvana could go with me to the hospital later on."

"I need Nirvana myself," said Mrs. Brown. "She has to stay with me after church at the lunch for the Women's Auxiliary. Maybe you should give your mother a little time, anyway."

"I want to see her," I insisted.

"Well, your big brother can go with you. You and Otis know where the hospital is."

I nodded. "We can make it on our own," I murmured. "No problem."

Two cats edged out on either side of her legs. Mrs. Brown bent down and carefully scooped them up.

"You can come over anytime," she offered.

"Thank you," I said, inching backward.

She trundled into her apartment with a cat under each arm. "Reckon your brother can take care of things for a little while. He's fifteen, after all. That is, if he can keep himself off the street. I see him hanging out there, you know. I see him from the window," she muttered. "Hopefully, your mother won't be gone that long. I'll sure pray for her...."

I ran down the stairs and out to the street, heading toward the singing teacher's. The sky was the same brilliant blue it had been on my birthday, but it didn't make me cheerful when I looked up. I put my head down and took off. Up the block at the newsstand, people were buying the newspaper. Outside the bagel store, there was a long line. On the corner, the smell of fresh doughnuts wafted out of Rivera's. As I was crossing the street, a man who had lost his legs scooted by me on a low platform with wheels. His arms looked strong. He glanced up and smiled at me. The lady who slept next to her cart was still there when I cut through the park. A cool breeze lifted, and my heart fluttered horribly. I was hanging tough, but still thinking of Ma.

When I arrived at the fancy brick house, I heard piano music coming out of the windows, and this time someone was singing. The song was jaunty, with lots of words that reminded me of something on Broadway. The voice was a man's, really deep. I sat down on the gray stone stairs and pulled out my thesaurus. I found a word for the sound: *sonorous.* Then I sat there, waiting for the singing lesson to be over. The day before, the teacher had said he had a slew of students; I hoped that this morning was different.

As soon as the singing stopped, I jumped up to ring the bell. Before I could, the door opened. An extremely fine-looking young man with a mustache and beard slid past. His eyes were gleaming. The singing teacher stood at the door.

"See you next week, Win," he called.

"See you, Jackson."

Jackson gave the young man a wave and then turned to me. "Glad you could come back, Mahalia." His eyes twinkled. I couldn't help smiling. He'd remembered my name.

"Is the job still open?"

He nodded. "I'm not sure it's the job for you, though. How do you feel about a lot of lifting and lugging?"

"I'm strong," I said, looking him in the eye. "In wood shop, I carry around big planks."

"You'd be getting your hands a little dirty," he added with a grin.

"I wouldn't mind that," I assured him. "Where's the yard? Does it have any flowers?"

He held up his thumb and chuckled. "Does this thumb look green or brown to you?"

"Brown," I allowed.

"There's your answer," he said good-naturedly. "But you're welcome to take a look at it. Go around the side of the house. I'll walk through and meet you out there."

I edged my way along the side of the house. "Come on around," I heard the singing teacher call out. I stepped around into the yard. My mouth dropped open.

Every inch of the good-sized rectangular space was covered with things: old doors, busted shutters, rusted-out screens, burlap bags, broken flowerpots, stacks of rotting wood. On one side of the yard was a rickety-looking shed, stuffed to overflowing. On the other side, toward the back, was a huge pile of stones. The property along the fence was completely overgrown with weeds. And what was left of the lawn was burned out, as if a chemical had been dropped on it! There were certainly no flowers to speak of. The house was so fancy. It seemed a shame that the yard was such a wreck. The one nice thing that I could see was a leafy old tree growing right in the middle.

"The tree's pretty," I murmured politely.

He rubbed his chin. "I suppose you want to know what happened to the rest of it."

"What did happen?"

"Ever had a messy room?" he asked.

I thought of our apartment that morning, before Otis and I had cleaned. "Yeah."

"Well, the inside of my house is pretty neat, because I kept all of my mess out here," he explained. "I used the yard for a kind of storage place when the inside of the house was being fixed up. I'd always meant to fix up the outside, too, but then I got sidetracked."

"But now you want to make a garden?" I ventured.

"That's more than I can hope for in the time that I've got," he said. "I've got students coming here for lessons nearly every day. That's why I was hoping to hire someone."

"I can take a crack at it," I offered.

He shook his head. "Look at these doors," he said. "Look at these big stones. I'm not sure you could manage it."

"I told you, I'm strong." I walked over to the stone pile and lifted a big stone off the top. I picked it up over my head and held it there.

"You didn't tell me that you were a weight lifter, Mahalia," he teased.

I grinned and put the stone down. "Call me Haley the Strong."

"Call me Jackson the Slob." He chuckled. "How old are you?"

"Thirteen."

He looked surprised.

"I'm small for my age," I explained. "Most people think that I'm younger."

"On the contrary," he said. "I thought that you were older."

"Really?"

"Your face is very mature, and you're quite poised. I teach in a middle school during the school year. I know my teenagers."

"Thanks," I said, blushing. It was the first time that

I'd been called a teenager! "So, do I have the job?"

"I'd like to hire you," Jackson said hesitantly, "but my daughter, Brielle, is coming home in about three weeks. I promised her that we'd have a barbecue. So I need the yard fixed up by then."

"Three weeks, huh?" I rubbed my hands together. "The first thing I'd do would be to get rid of the junk."

"I'd have to get it out front somehow," said Jackson, "so that I could arrange for a pickup from a rubbish company. I might have time to help drag out some of the heavier stuff." He looked around at the mess. "There might be some things worth saving or storing in the shed."

"The shed is full," I pointed out.

"Maybe the person I hire can make room," he muttered.

I looked down at the ground. "What about grass?"

"Too late for that," said Jackson.

"What about flowers?" I piped up. "My favorites are tulips."

"Definitely too late for flowers," he said matter-of-factly.

"If there's no grass or flowers, all you'll have left is dirt."

He stuck his hands into his pockets. "That's okay. My grandmother had a dirt yard."

I wrinkled my nose. "A dirt yard?"

"A dirt yard can be great," he countered. "You'd have to pull up all this dead grass, of course, and then do a lot of raking. A dirt yard is a great workplace."

"What kind of work?" I asked curiously.

"Peeling potatoes," he replied. "Sawing wood, stuff like that. If you have a dirt yard, you throw things on the ground and then sweep up."

"Sweep the ground?" I asked in amazement.

Jackson laughed. "My grandmother swept her yard every evening—honest! She said it was her way of putting her mind at rest. The universe could be exploding, but if Grandma's yard was swept, she felt just fine."

I lifted an eyebrow. "If you say so."

"What happens to these?" I asked, pointing to the pile of stones. The stones were a pale gray color, of varying shapes and sizes. No two seemed exactly alike.

Jackson shrugged. "Maybe I can get somebody with a truck to take them."

I picked up one of the smaller stones and ran my finger across it. The surface was bumpy and had tiny white sparkling specks in it. "This one looks like it has diamonds in it," I mused. "Where did you get these stones?"

"Oh, I didn't carry them in," Jackson said with a chuckle. He pointed to the ground. "They came from right here. Once upon a time, they were buried beneath the earth."

"Did you dig them up?"

"Not me," he said. "Some farmer, more than likely. They're fieldstones. People had to dig up a lot of stones before they could plow their fields and grow things."

I glanced around at the houses surrounding us. "But there aren't any fields around here."

"This whole area used to be farms a few hundred years ago," Jackson informed me.

It was hard to imagine. I shook my head. "Wow, these stones have been in this spot for hundreds of years?"

"Some farmer probably used them to build a stone wall. Of course, the wall collapsed long before I got here."

"Maybe you can build another stone wall," I suggested.

"You have to be an expert to build a stone wall," Jackson said. "Besides, my daughter will be here before I know it. I have to do something quickly."

"I don't want to be nosy," I ventured, "but hasn't she seen the stones before?"

"Oh, she's seen them," said Jackson, "but not for a while. When she's not in college in California, she lives with her mother. Her mother lives out that way, too."

"I thought maybe she lived here with you," I said in surprise. "I figured that she was just away at summer camp."

He chuckled. "Brielle is too old for summer camp," he said. "Are you going to camp this summer?"

"I wish I could," I admitted. "My friend from school is going. But this year my family can't afford it."

"Have you ever been?" asked Jackson.

I shook my head.

"Too bad," he said kindly.

"That's okay." I gave him a cheerful smile. "I'm hoping to get a summer job instead."

"I hope you do get a chance to go to camp one year," he added. "When she was younger, Brielle used to love it. Now she works most of her summers. I can't believe it," he added wistfully. "She's almost twenty."

Jackson ran a hand over his thinning dark curls. "When we first moved into this house, I was so excited by the space out here. I wanted to make it a little piece of heaven...." His voice trailed off as he circled the yard.

"So, what do you think?" he piped up again. "Can we make something out of it?"

My heart beat with excitement. He had said *we*. "We can try. I really need a job."

"You're hired, then. I'll pay you five dollars an hour."

"Great! When do I get started?"

"Whenever you'd like," said Jackson. "Give me your telephone number. I'll call your parents."

"My mother will call you," I said hastily. "And my dad doesn't live with us."

"I see," he said. "Sorry."

"It's okay, really." I lowered my eyes. "I hardly ever think about him."

For an instant, I thought Jackson looked sad. "I'll go inside and write down my telephone number for your mom, then," he said, hurrying away. The back entrance was a pair of glass doors. "Grab that old lawn chair next to the shed," he called before going inside. "Sit down, if you like."

He ducked into the house. I peered through the glass after him. He walked into a large room with a huge piano right in the middle and tall bookcases lining the walls; then he disappeared around a corner. *Imagine having your own huge piano!* I thought. *Imagine owning all of those books on the shelves! Imagine living all by yourself in a house three stories high!* I stepped back. Working for Jackson would be like

working for a king, I thought dreamily. A king who was await-
ing the return of his long-lost princess. The princess's name
was Brielle. And I was the royal gardener, Mistress Haley. I
chuckled out loud and strolled toward the shed. I found the
old lawn chair and set it under the tree. The tree had tiny
white buds on it that gave off a nice fragrance. I sniffed and
took a seat. The fluttering in my heart had calmed down. I
could hardly wait to tell Ma that I had a real job.

Jackson came back outside carrying two glasses of iced
tea.

"Thought you'd like a drink on a hot day like this," he
said, offering me one of them.

"Thanks," I said, licking my lips. My mouth was
parched. I gulped the tea down. It had just the right amount
of sugar in it.

He glanced around at the yard. "I really did let things get
out of hand back here," he muttered.

"Don't worry," I said, draining the last of my tea. "I'll
have this place fixed up in no time. You'll see!"

He smiled broadly. "I don't doubt it for a minute, Haley."

At three o'clock on the dot, I stood in the lobby of the hospital. I'd been there before when I'd dropped in on Ma at

her job. When Grandma Dora had been in the hospital, I'd been too young to visit her. I walked up to the big circular desk in the middle of the first floor. When I'd visited Ma on the job, I'd always told them I was going up to the second floor to Admitting. Now, I wasn't quite sure what to say. I cleared my throat.

"May I help you?" the receptionist asked kindly. I didn't recognize her.

"I'm going to visit my mother," I explained. "You might know her. Her name is Eva Moon. She works in Admitting. But now she's a patient."

"Sorry, I don't know her," the woman said. She pushed a book across the desk. "Are you thirteen?"

I nodded.

"Sign in, please. I'll look up your mother's room number on the computer."

I signed my name and swallowed nervously. Suppose the receptionist found a reason why I couldn't visit Ma?

"Room four-oh-three," she said, giving me a visitor's card.

I breathed a sigh of relief.

"The first elevator bank," she directed me, pointing.

I walked across the lobby. A few people were seated in big

leather chairs. The hospital had never seemed so large before. I got into the elevator with a woman and a man, both dressed in white coats like doctors. When I got off on four, the hallway was empty, though I could hear the sound of a television coming from one of the rooms. I stepped forward and squinted at the number on one of the closed doors.

"Looking for someone?" a woman asked. She stood behind a circular desk a little farther down the hall. She had dark hair and a young face.

"Eva Moon," I said. My voice echoed. "I'm her daughter."

The young woman smiled reassuringly. "Your mother asked me to be on the lookout. Said her kids might be coming." She led me to room 403. The door was half open. I could see Ma sitting in a chair, her back to me. The young nurse disappeared. I knocked and walked in.

"Hey, Ma."

She turned. When I saw her, I felt like crying. Her face was very swollen. I went over and gave her a hug. She was wearing a green blouse that I liked, and she smelled like soap. I noticed her hair was nicely combed.

"I've been waiting for you, baby girl," she said, almost in a whisper. "Where is your brother?"

"Otis couldn't make it," I apologized. "He had to work."

I glanced around the room. Everything in it was white. It was nice and cool.

"You have air-conditioning!" I exclaimed.

Ma nodded. "Pretty luxurious, huh?" Her eyes were red. "Under different circumstances, it would be a nice vacation spot."

"Does the food taste okay?" I asked, trying to sound cheerful.

"I haven't been able to eat much." She plucked a white tissue out of a box on the stand next to the chair.

"I got a job," I said brightly.

"A job!" she said. "Is it a baby-sitting job?"

I smiled like the cat that had swallowed the canary. "I'm a yard helper."

"And just what is a yard helper?" asked Ma in a nervous voice.

I perched on the edge of the bed across from her. "I'm helping a singing teacher fix up his backyard. His daughter, Brielle, is coming home and he wants everything to be perfect for her. He's such a nice man," I gushed. "And I think his students sing on Broadway and in the opera."

Ma fiddled with her ring that had belonged to Grandma Dora. "Did Otis meet him? Did you tell Mrs. Brown?"

"Not yet," I replied. I took the telephone number out of my pocket. "He said you could call him." I held out the piece of paper.

She shook her head. "I don't know, Haley…."

"I have to take the job, Ma," I pressed. "I told him already. I'm getting five dollars an hour."

"That's good money for a kid your age," she admitted. "But the thought of you running all over town, while I'm in here…." She made a helpless gesture with her hands. "Why can't you just stay inside and read?"

"I'm not going to stay inside all day long," I protested. "It's summertime. This is my summer job, Ma."

Ma slid down in her chair. She pressed her fingers into the middle of her forehead and closed her eyes hard. She stayed that way for at least five minutes, without moving a muscle. My heart started fluttering again. It was scary.

"Did you have a nervous breakdown, Ma?" I asked quietly.

Tears were rolling down her cheeks when she took her hands away. "I hope not," she said, with her voice shaking. "The doctor is trying me on different medications."

My stomach knotted up. "Can you try them out at home?"

She shook her head. "I can't. I can't do that to you and Otis. Besides, I can't handle it alone." Ma wiped her cheeks, but the tears kept on flowing. I glanced away. I couldn't stand watching.

"What are we supposed to do, Ma?" I whispered.

She stood up, struggling to compose herself. "Be good," she said. She came close. She touched my hair next to my face. "Go home now. I'm not so sure that you should come back."

"But I want to come back. Please, Ma. I'll come tomorrow after my job," I promised hurriedly. "My boss, Jackson, has a garden with no flowers. He wants a dirt yard, isn't that funny?" I said with a nervous laugh.

"What he needs is flower bulbs," she said, staring off into space. I patted her back. Why was she acting this way? It was as if my strong Ma had turned into paper.

"You're not to come back here," she said, turning to me abruptly. "Do you hear me? You have to let me get well."

"But how can I talk to you?" I breathed.

"You can keep in touch by telephone," she said. "You can call me every day. It's the best thing, Haley."

Then she kissed me good-bye.

I drifted out of the room and down the hallway. A knife of pain went through me. Why had this happened to my mother?

CHAPTER FOUR

Our apartment smelled like a dead rat. Otis and I looked for it everywhere, under the kitchen sink and in the closet. Finally, our noses led us to the stove.

"I think it's in the oven," I said squeamishly.

Otis picked up the broom and inched forward.

"Don't tell me you're afraid of a dead rat," I teased.

"Aren't you?" he challenged. "Some of those rats are as big as dogs. I've seen them over in the vacant lot."

"But this one is dead," I pointed out. "If it's dead, it can't hurt us."

He grabbed the handle of the oven door, and I leaped out of the way.

"Look who's chicken now," Otis muttered with a smirk.

A wave of stench hit us in the face.

"Something dead is in there, all right," Otis pronounced, making a face.

I held my nose and peeked in. The dead "rat" turned out to be "dead" duck *à l'orange*, which had been rotting in the oven since the night of my birthday. Otis howled hysterically. I have to admit, I thought it was funny myself. There we were, shaking in our boots over what we thought was a ferocious rodent, when all the time it was only a helpless little duck smothered with rotten oranges. I got out a garbage bag and Otis tossed the whole thing in, even Ma's baking pan. All the way to the garbage chute, we couldn't stop laughing.

When I told the story to Ma on the phone that night, she didn't think it was funny at all. In fact, it made her sadder than ever.

"Poor Haley!" she sobbed into the telephone. "Poor Otis!"

"Stop crying," I pleaded. "We're fine. It wasn't a rat. It was a duck."

"But that was your birthday duck!" she moaned. She cried some more.

It was almost as if Ma was looking for things to be upset about. Still, every evening I called her.

"Otis and I cooked some beans," I told her on the telephone once. She always wanted to know what we ate.

"Did you soak them first?" she asked quietly.

"Nope. But we cooked them for seven hours."

I heard her sigh.

"Don't worry, Ma. They tasted good. The only problem was that they kept on expanding. First we put them into a little pot, but then we had to find a pot that was bigger. The same thing happened to the rice. I never knew how much rice and beans expand when you cook them." I giggled. "Food was everywhere."

"What do you mean?" she asked in alarm.

"Both of the pots boiled over, even the big ones. The rice and beans just wouldn't stop cooking. It was like the story of the porridge."

"Porridge?" she sounded confused. "You ate cereal with rice and beans?"

"No, Ma," I pressed, "the story of the porridge in *Grimms'*. You used to read it to me," I reminded her. "The porridge filled up the whole town, so everyone had to eat their way out?"

"This isn't a fairy tale," she said with a whimper. "I don't want to hear this."

"We ended up throwing most of it out, anyway," I said quietly.

She cleared her throat. "Where was Mrs. Brown?"

"At home watching television."

"Does she ever bring you anything for dinner?" Ma asked helplessly.

"She brought us some turnip greens and ham hocks. Don't worry, Ma, we aren't starving."

Ma began to wail. "I hate those fatty ham hocks!"

She cried and cried, so I finally hung up.

If I mentioned Otis on the telephone, that was a sure cue for her to break up. But Ma always wanted to hear about him.

"Where's your brother? What is he up to?" she asked one night.

"He leaves early every morning and travels around with his buddy Reggie."

She drew in a breath. "Where does he go?"

"I don't know. He and his partner set up their incense stand down in the subway. He always comes home after dark."

"That boy…he'd better not be up to anything," she muttered. "I've got to get home to check up on him."

"You're coming home?" I asked. "When?"

"I'm not sure," she answered. "The doctor is trying to adjust the medication." Her voice drifted off.

I pressed my ear to the phone. She was trying to hold

it in this time, but I could still hear her crying softly.

She even cried when I told her about my blister! "I was lifting rocks in Jackson's yard," I reported. "I got a big blister on one of my pinkies."

Ma burst into tears like a baby.

"Snap out of it, Ma," I said, losing my patience. "It wasn't *your* blister, it was *my* blister. All I needed was a little bandage."

Otis never talked to Ma himself, but I reported it all to him faithfully.

"If she doesn't stop all that crying, she might go blind," my brother said, pacing the floor.

"People don't go blind from crying," I told him. "But she might feel better if you called her."

"Not until she acts like herself again," declared Otis. "Anyway, she'll be nagging me."

Even though I knew that people don't go blind from crying, I wasn't so sure they might not mentally drown. It was as if Ma had fallen into a well, a well of tears that she couldn't climb out of. Her voice had such a faraway sound! When we talked on the phone, I felt as if I were calling down the well to her. If I had had long braids, like Rapunzel, I could have made a ladder for Ma to climb up on. But she wasn't in a well, and I didn't have braids, and if I had thrown my braids down to Ma, she would probably have pulled me in with her. I wondered if depression was catching. Sometimes after I talked with her, I felt blue, too. Not exactly as if I were in a well, more as if I were in a moat or a chilly bog....

If talking to Ma made me feel bog-like, working for Jackson was like standing on hot, dry land. I never imagined how hard it would be to move a door. There were eight of them stacked up in the yard. It took me one whole morning to move them. Jackson had said that he would help during breaks between singing students, but I wanted to do it alone to surprise him. The hardest part was figuring out how. They were too heavy to lift, that's for sure. So I had to push each one a little at a time off the top of the stack, and then when I had just enough door hanging over one side, I would tilt it so that it was standing straight up. Then I wiggled it toward the fence, where I would rest it at an angle. I moved eight doors that way and lined them up. But the doors had to be carried a lot farther than that. Jackson had a rubbish company coming at the end of the week. The company had agreed to pick up the doors and some other stuff, but the things had to be out front. I didn't have to carry the doors down the stone stairs, but I still had to get them along the side of the house somehow. I found the answer in the shed: an old pair of steel roller skates, a board, a hammer, nails, and some wire. I punched some holes into the board with the hammer and nails and placed the roller skates beneath it. Then I threaded the wire through the holes and around the skates, fastening them on to make a rolling platform. I needed a rope to pull it with, but I settled for a piece of burlap bag, which I nailed onto the front. Then, one at a time, I tilted the doors onto the platform and pulled them around the house and out front.

Meanwhile, through the open windows, I could hear Jackson's students singing. Not all of Jackson's students had voices as good as Win's, the boy with the deep voice that I'd heard a few days before. One boy singing the scales couldn't seem to find the right note. A girl who sang well low cracked on the high parts. Two students sounded okay, but I couldn't understand the words to their songs. I think that they were in Spanish or Italian. When I sneaked a few peeks through the glass doors, everybody looked cheerful, even the ones who'd messed up.

Around noon, Jackson came out for a break. I stood in the middle of the yard, smiling. "What have you done?" he asked, glancing around. "Something's different."

"The doors are gone," I announced.

"How?" he asked in surprise.

I pointed to my platform.

"You made a moving dolly," he exclaimed. "Amazing!"

"I told you I took wood shop."

"Great job," said Jackson. "Those doors weigh a ton. How about a break?"

I went inside and washed my hands in the kitchen while he made us some sandwiches.

"How's that blister?" he asked.

"Almost gone," I said, drying my finger gingerly.

He smiled and shook his head. "I had my doubts about whether you'd be able to handle this job. You're pretty strong."

"My arms and back are sore," I admitted.

"Try soaking in a hot bath tonight," he suggested.

He spread some peanut butter on four slices of bread. I opened the refrigerator and took out some milk. I'd only worked there for a little while, but I already felt at home.

"Your mom called me last night," said Jackson, getting me a glass.

I lifted an eyebrow. I hoped that she hadn't been crying. "Sorry it took her so long," I apologized.

He peered at me. "I didn't know that she was in the hospital."

"She went in kind of suddenly," I muttered. "I didn't think it mattered, so I didn't bring it up."

"Of course it doesn't matter, as far as your working for me is concerned," he said, plopping the sandwiches onto a plate. "I just hope that your mother's illness isn't too serious."

I straightened my shoulders. "She'll be home soon. She's just a little depressed."

"Are you staying with a relative?" he asked.

"My brother, Otis. He's an entrepreneur."

He picked up the plate. "Your mother must be very proud. She's got two industrious kids."

"Guess so," I muttered, taking a sip of my milk.

"This summer, Brielle is working on a movie set," Jackson said. "She wants to be a filmmaker someday."

My eyes popped. "Wow, she must be creative."

"She always was," he said. "You're pretty creative yourself, I bet."

We went out to the yard. Jackson managed to locate another decrepit lawn chair in the shed to match the one that was already out. We sat down to eat.

Jackson glanced around the yard. "You've really made

some headway, Haley. I feel kind of guilty spending the days indoors teaching, while you're slugging away at it out here."

"I like seeing the fruits of my labor," I said, munching my sandwich.

Jackson chuckled. "That dolly you built was clever. So, is woodworking one of your hobbies?"

I rolled my eyes. "I haven't done very much outside of school. My main hobby is reading."

"What kinds of things do you like to read?" he asked.

My neck got hot. I figured that Jackson liked to read himself, since he had a ton of books. "I like to read fairy tales," I confessed. I waited for a weird look.

"I like them, too," he said brightly.

"You're kidding!" I exclaimed. "People are supposed to outgrow fairy tales. My mother keeps waiting for me to read older books. She even gave me this," I said, pulling out my thesaurus.

"A thesaurus! How great!"

"Actually, I love it myself," I said. "I have a thing for interesting words. My brother hates it. He thinks I'm too loquacious, especially when I'm insulting him."

Jackson's eyes twinkled. "What's your brother's name again?"

"Otis."

"Like Otis Redding?"

I nodded. Ma told me that Dad had dreamed up Otis's name.

"How old is your brother?" asked Jackson.

"Fifteen."

He glanced at me sharply. "And you're staying by yourselves while your mother is in the hospital?"

I shrugged. "We can manage. We've got a neighbor, Mrs. Brown, who checks in on us."

"I guess Otis could handle pretty much anything that arises," Jackson commented. "It's amazing how capable some fifteen-year-olds are these days."

I giggled. "I'm not sure that *capable* is exactly the adjective I'd use for my brother. He *can* be enterprising," I added, not wanting to give Otis a bad name.

"I don't want to butt in, but if I can ever do anything…"

I nodded. "Thanks. But we'll be okay."

Jackson gave me a thoughtful smile. "I'll bet you anything that you're the capable one in your family."

I rolled my eyes. "I've let a few pots boil over on the stove since Ma's been gone."

He chuckled. "Why worry about being a good cook,

when you can build a moving dolly? I bet you can even sing," he said, popping down the last of his sandwich.

"I sing alto in the school chorus," I volunteered, "but most of all, I like listening to music. I love to listen to your students while I work."

"Some of my students are just beginners," he said. "This morning you heard some pretty unpolished stuff. But it's amazing what they'll sound like in a year or so."

"When you were playing the piano the first day I came, I got goose bumps on my arms," I blurted out. "I could listen to that forever."

"There you go, complimenting me again," he said modestly. "Being able to listen is a gift, too. Not everyone can respond deeply to music." He got up and stretched. "What an improvement, having those doors out of the way! Sorry I wasn't able to help you."

"I was fine by myself," I said staunchly.

"I'm sure you were," said Jackson. A smile flitted across his lips. "I've been dreaming of the little party I'm planning for Brielle out here. Looks like it might happen."

"Is it her birthday?" I asked curiously.

"No, her birthday is in April." He touched one of the leaves on the tree. "This is more of a homecoming celebration."

I imagined a tall, pretty girl with slicked-back hair walking into the yard, carrying a movie camera. Brielle and Jackson would hug each other, and then she'd make a movie starring her father. The movie set would be a garden with green grass and flowers, a garden that I had created in the yard! Though Jackson and Brielle wouldn't see me, I'd be there, too, hiding behind the tree, perhaps.

"When my mother comes home, I think I'll give her a homecoming party, too," I piped up.

"That's a wonderful idea," said Jackson. "I've always loved giving parties."

The doorbell rang.

"Back to work!" he exclaimed, hurrying away. "One of my older students."

I stretched my arms and crossed to the stack of old shutters. The sun was beating down overhead. Sneaking a peek over my shoulder through the glass doors, I watched Jackson's student. She was the same one who had come for a lesson on the very first day I'd met Jackson. He played a grand introduction and the girl's gorgeous soprano voice soared. She sang with a huge smile on her face. I went to work.

Over the next few days, I filled up bag after bag with rubble and pieces of old wood, while listening to Jackson's students. I divided their voices into two categories: *mellifluous*, for the sweet ones, and *cracked*, for the ones that couldn't carry a tune. After the garbage bags were stacked in a corner of the yard to wait until collection day, and the stuff for the special rubbish collector was all out front, most of the yard was actually cleared! Unfortunately, in the spots where grass should have been, there were burned-out patches of crud instead. It looked like the scene of a forest fire....

Jackson had asked me to store some screens in the shed, but there was no room. I decided to take everything out and sort it into piles, so that Jackson could see what he had. I thought I would never get through it.

There were cans of dried-out paint, stacks of flowerpots, curtain rods, and bags of damp, smelly grass seed; a tangled-up rainbow-colored hammock, a perfectly good sewing machine covered with grime, and a barbecue grill with an amputated leg.

Near the back of the shed, things got even more interesting: Christmas ornaments, stuffed animals, and old-fashioned costumes! I even found an ancient telephone that you had to dial instead of pushing a button. I also counted ten pairs of candlestick holders! And at least six boxes of sheet music, not to mention a box of books that had gotten all moldy. Beyond it all, wedged in the farthest corner, were a green tricycle and a pink tutu, which I guessed must have belonged to Brielle. I found a spot for them on the lawn, along with everything else. When Jackson came outside during his break, he was shocked. Now that every inch of lawn was covered again, all of our headway seemed to have disappeared.

"What is all this?" he asked in a panicky voice. "Where did it come from? It looks like a flea market."

I pointed to the shed. "It belongs to you."

"Are you kidding?" he exclaimed. "I haven't seen this stuff in years. I'd forgotten I had it."

"Jackson the Slob."

He laughed. "Thanks for reminding me."

"So, what should I do with these things?" I asked, peeking into the box of stuffed animals.

"I'm not sure," he murmured. "I hate to throw it away. Once upon a time, there was a use for all these things, but now..."

"Maybe somebody else could use some of the stuff," I suggested. I glanced at the box filled with candlestick holders. "Guess you used to burn a lot of candles."

"The candlesticks weren't my idea," he said with a chuckle. "I had an aunt Laurie who had a poor memory. Every year for Christmas, she sent me the same thing. Gosh," he added with a sigh, "maybe we should put all this clutter into garbage bags and leave it out for the trash pickup."

"What about the barbecue grill?" I remarked. "I found the missing leg. You could put it back on. A barbecue grill kind of goes with a backyard."

"I'll need a grill for the cookout with Brielle," he agreed. "Let's see if we can fix it."

"And don't tell me that you're going to throw these away?" I said, fishing through the box of Christmas ornaments. I pulled out a string of tiny Christmas tree lights. "You could put these on your tree next year."

"I don't get a tree anymore," said Jackson.

"How come?"

He shrugged. "Nobody to see it but me."

"What about Brielle?"

"Brielle doesn't visit me very much."

"Not even at Christmas?"

"She doesn't feel very comfortable here," he said sadly, "because of the divorce. That's why this visit coming up is so important."

I shook my head in disbelief. As far as I was concerned, Jackson's home was like a castle. I couldn't imagine staying away if my father had a home like that.

"Your mom and dad must have gone through something like that," Jackson added.

"That was different," I blurted out. "My dad wasn't like you."

"What is your father like?" Jackson asked.

"He could be nice. I'm not sure," I said hesitantly. "It's been a long time since I've seen him."

I crouched down on the ground and stared at all the stuff. Both of us were quiet for a moment. "So, what's the verdict? Do we toss it all out?" I asked, breaking the silence.

"Toss out the things that are too far gone to be fixed," he said decisively. "Bag up the rest for the Salvation Army. And if there's anything that you can use at your house, feel free to take it."

I perked up. "Really?"

"Pretend you're at a free flea market," Jackson quipped.

"I'll take one of these," I decided, scooting over to the box of stuffed animals. I pulled out a long-legged monkey. "I can't believe it!" I exclaimed. "My neighbor Nirvana has a monkey just like this! She made him talk when she used to baby-sit me." I hugged the toy. "He's so cute. Does he have a name?"

Jackson grinned. "His name is Monkey."

"Nirvana named hers Monkey, too!" I squealed.

We both laughed. "I guess it's a pretty logical name," I added sheepishly.

"Monkey was one of Brielle's favorite things," said Jackson.

"And she left him," I said. "Too bad."

"She'll be glad to know that he's been adopted," he assured me. Jackson paused at the tutu and the tricycle.

"Maybe we should keep these two things," he added thoughtfully. "Brielle might want them for her own kids someday."

"I'll put the tricycle back in the shed," I offered. When I came back, Jackson had picked up the tutu.

"Did you ever take ballet?" he asked.

"I wanted to," I said, "but we couldn't afford it. We're supposed to be saving our extra money for a trip to Disney World, but we haven't gotten there yet. Did Brielle take dance classes?" I asked.

"Along with a million other things, when she moved to

California. Her mother tells me that Brielle has a lot of interests. But I guess now she's settled on moviemaking." He looked at his watch. "Ten more minutes and Shari will be here."

"I love her voice."

"I hate to leave you with all this stuff again," he apologized.

I swung my fists playfully. "Just let me at it!"

Jackson laughed. "Confident, aren't you? You're like that little tailor in *Grimms'*."

I chuckled. "You mean the one who got seven in one blow?"

He winked. "Told you I know my fairy tales."

I smiled. "I hope I can knock off the junk in this yard, the way the tailor knocked off those flies."

"I'm sure you can," he said. "You sure you won't take something else home?"

"Maybe a candlestick holder for my neighbor Mrs. Brown."

"Take all of them," Jackson said, waving his hand.

"Ma might be able to use those Christmas tree lights," I added. "I'll show them to her when she comes home from the hospital."

"How is your mother?" Jackson asked.

"I'm not sure," I confessed.

"Do you and Otis visit her at the hospital?" he wanted to know.

I lowered my eyes. "She doesn't want us to," I said with a swallow.

"That must be hard for you," Jackson said kindly.

"She'll only let me talk with her on the telephone," I blurted out. "No matter what, she always ends up crying. That's the way depression is, I guess."

"There are so many ways of treating it nowadays," Jackson pointed out. "I'm sure her doctors will find a way to help."

"They haven't yet," I said grimly. I looked up at him. "I wish you could have met my mother before she got this way. She's the kind of person who never lets anything get her down. She put herself through night school while holding down a job and taking care of Otis and me."

"I bet she's a great person," said Jackson.

"Want to see what she looks like?" I asked. I impulsively pulled out my wallet and opened it to a picture of Ma and Otis. It was one of my favorites of Ma. She was dressed in a soft blue outfit with a ruffled collar, standing on the steps outside

Grandma Dora's. Otis was standing next to her, with a crooked smile on his face. Jackson peered at the photograph.

"Your mother glows," Jackson exclaimed. "Look at that smile!"

"That's Ma all over," I said wistfully.

"And that's Otis?"

I nodded.

Jackson's eyes twinkled. "I bet he's got a sense of humor."

"He's a rogue," I said mischievously. I put the picture away.

"I'd like to meet them," Jackson said.

"I'm sure you will," I promised, "when Ma gets well and Otis isn't so busy with his incense stand."

He turned to the door and beckoned to me. "Now it's my turn. Come on in. I'll show you a picture of Brielle."

I followed him inside.

"Here she is," he said, producing a small framed picture from the edge of the piano. The picture was of a beautiful little girl with huge dark eyes and curly dark hair just like Jackson's. She'd lost her two front teeth. Just looking at her made me grin.

"It was taken when she was seven," Jackson said, putting the picture carefully in its place.

The same thing Jackson had said about Ma could be said about the girl in the picture. She glowed. I peeked at Jackson's face. He missed Brielle a lot. I could tell. Maybe as much as I missed Ma. *What could have kept him and his daughter apart?* I wondered. But now that Brielle was coming to visit, all of that would be over.

Jackson laid a hand on my shoulder. "When your mom gets out of the hospital, we'll have a barbecue for her, too. And I hope that Otis will come."

"Really?" I gazed up at him.

"Really," he promised.

The doorbell rang. Jackson let Shari inside. Today her hair was in tiny dreadlocks, and she was wearing yellow pants, an orange blouse, and bright red lipstick. Her eyes were bright.

"This is my friend Mahalia," Jackson said, introducing me.

Shari smiled. "That's the name of my mom's favorite singer," she said in a lilting voice. "Mahalia Jackson. She was a star. She sang gospels and spirituals. Check out her recordings. That's your two names together," Shari pointed out with a grin.

Jackson beamed at me. "What do you know? Must be destiny."

The lesson began, and I wandered back into the yard. "*Destiny...*" I murmured the word aloud. It was a word I liked.

At home that night, I took a hot bath. Otis was out later than usual. I made myself an egg sandwich for dinner and put on my blue pajamas. Even though I was at home, I felt homesick. Homesick for Ma. I pulled the telephone over to the table and made my evening call.

"Hi, Ma."

"Hi, sweetie."

"Are you better today?"

"I think so."

"Did the medicine help?" I asked hopefully.

"Yes. I feel different."

She sounded different, too. She wasn't crying.

"I got some Christmas tree lights from Jackson," I told her eagerly. "I'm saving them for you. He gave me some candlestick holders for Mrs. Brown."

"He sounds like a nice man." She wasn't crying, but her voice was very quiet.

"I can't hear you very well, Ma."

"Sorry," she said, speaking up a bit.

"I did a lot of work on the yard," I reported. "I made lots of money."

"That's good, Haley."

"Hey, Ma, do you know who Mahalia Jackson is?"

"She was a great singer," she said softly. "Your father named you for her, don't you remember?"

My eyes welled up with tears. "You never told me that."

"Sure, I did. You must have forgotten."

Why did I feel like crying, when for once Ma wasn't crying at all? I bit my lip.

"Coming home soon, Ma?" I asked, changing the subject.

"I'm trying, Haley. I'm trying."

CHAPTER FIVE

When I woke up the next morning, it was pouring buckets of rain. Otis had come in after I'd fallen asleep, but he was already up and standing over me waving a long white glittery dress. "What's going on?" I asked, rubbing my eyes. "Where did that come from?"

He grinned. "Like it?"

"Who does it belong to?"

"It's yours, if you want it," he said.

I sat up. Otis let the dress drop into my lap. "I love it," I said with a little gasp. The dress was fitted on top and had a full, swirling skirt, with lots of layers and sparkly white sequins. I stood up and put it on over my pajamas.

"Not bad," said Otis. "It'll look better without your blue pajama sleeves showing."

I ran across the room to look at myself in the mirror. That's when I noticed the rest of the clothes piled in Ma's alcove.

"What is all this?" I said in amazement. Dresses, suits,

and jackets were stacked all over Ma's bed, most of them still covered in plastic. The place looked like a dry cleaner's. "Where did these things come from?"

Otis shrugged. "From my partner, Reggie. I hate to tell you how much these threads cost," he added, holding a suit up in front of himself.

"You bought all this?" I asked in alarm. "With Ma in the hospital, we have to watch what we spend. I'm saving everything I make for a rainy day."

"Today *is* a rainy day," Otis quipped. He patted me on the head. "Relax, Sis. I didn't buy these clothes. I'm holding this stuff for Reggie. You see, we sell clothes like this at our incense stand."

"People buy clothes at an incense stand?" I asked in confusion.

Otis smiled. "We branched out."

"Where do the clothes come from?" I asked.

"That's Reggie's department," said Otis. "I just sell them."

"Wow," I said, sifting through the clothes. "These look expensive. You and Reggie must be making a lot of money."

"Making a little change," Otis bragged.

"So am I," I couldn't help boasting. I pulled up one of my

pajama sleeves and flexed a bicep. "And look at my muscles! Working in Jackson's yard is getting me into shape."

Otis beamed. "I'm proud of you, Sis. Me and you aren't doing too bad on our own, right?"

"I still miss Ma," I admitted. "Don't you?"

"Yeah, I miss her. But it's nice not to have her trying to check up on my every move."

"Let's save up all the money we make and surprise her," I suggested eagerly. "When she gets out of the hospital, she won't have to worry about paying any bills. She'll be so proud of us."

"Think she'll be proud of me, too?" Otis asked skeptically.

"Of course she'll be proud of you," I assured him. "She always wanted you to get a job, and now you have a really good one. Ma is doing better," I reported. "Last night she wasn't crying."

Otis let out a little sigh. "That's a relief." He gave me a toothy smile. "Thanks for taking over like that for me with Ma. I'm older, so I guess I should be the one going to see her and calling her on the telephone. But it kind of bothers me when she acts like a nut."

"She's still our mother, Otis," I reminded him quietly. I

swished past the stack of clothes toward the window. Raindrops splashed off the fire escape and onto the windowsill. "Guess I have the day off," I said, breathing in the misty coolness. "How about you, Otis?" I called over my shoulder.

"Oh, we'll be out of the rain, down in the subway station," Otis assured me. "This should be a big day for us. Most people have Saturday off, so they'll be looking to buy stuff. And my man Reggie and I will be there to sell it to them."

"Here comes another working man," I announced, spying Dill McCoy running up the block.

Otis peeked out and chuckled. "Ol' burger flipper! The way he wears that restaurant uniform, you'd think he was in the military. And look at that tore-up umbrella he's carrying," my brother scoffed. "The dude doesn't have any style."

"I like him," I said, pushing Otis out of the way. "Hey, Dill!" I cried, poking my head out the window.

"Hi, little chick," he called up. He was coming to our building, just as I'd suspected.

"Tell Nirvana to stop over," I yelled down.

"Okay," he said, ducking inside.

"Why did you have to do that?" Otis grumbled. "All I need is them two over here."

"Don't be so grouchy," I countered. "I want to show my monkey and the candlestick holders to Nirvana."

"What monkey?" he demanded. "What candlestick holders?"

"That monkey," I said, pointing to where I'd placed the little stuffed animal at the top of my bed. "I got it from Jackson's," I explained. "He let me have some candlestick holders, too," I added, crossing to the shopping bag I'd left by the door.

There was a tap at the door. I opened it. Nirvana and Dill stood in the hallway.

"Grandma sent over some fresh muffins," Nirvana said, holding out a plate. She did a double take.

"Child, where did you get that dress? You look like a princess!"

"Thanks," I said, blushing.

Otis reached over me and grabbed a muffin. "I'll take one of those."

"Can we come in first?" Nirvana said pointedly.

"Of course," I said, opening the door wider.

Otis skulked across the room. "How much you want to bet there ain't no butter in this house?" he muttered. "Ma bought everything but the important stuff." He bit off half his muffin. "Tastes good," he said grudgingly.

Nirvana stepped inside and presented me with the plate. I took a deep sniff. "Smells like banana-nut muffins," I murmured. "Would you and Dill like one yourselves?" I asked.

"I've already eaten," said Dill.

"They're for you, Haley," Nirvana said graciously.

I put the muffins down on the table and picked one out. They were still warm. "Yum," I exclaimed, biting in. "It's delicious. Tell your grandma thank you for us."

"I will," said Nirvana.

Dill sauntered across the room to Ma's alcove, where all the clothes were stacked. He eyed Otis.

"Y'all opening a department store?" Dill muttered.

I laughed. "It looks that way, doesn't it? Those clothes don't belong to us. They belong to the incense stand."

Dill lifted an eyebrow. Meanwhile, Nirvana peeked into one of the garment bags and spotted a red-beaded gown.

"Look at this dress! It's gorgeous!"

"Must cost a fortune," Dill commented. He gave Otis a sidelong glance. "Not what you'd usually pick up at an incense stand."

"Mind your business, McCoy," Otis snapped with a scowl. He turned his attention to Nirvana and the red-beaded dress. "Go ahead, take it out."

Nirvana slipped the slinky dress out of its plastic. "This is outrageous!" she cried, holding the gown up to her body.

"You've got the body for it, baby," Otis observed.

Ignoring Otis's comment, Nirvana turned to Dill. "What do you think, honey?"

Dill grinned. "You look like one of those chicks on the Academy Awards."

"It's so beautiful," Nirvana murmured. "Of course, I wouldn't know where to wear a dress like this myself."

"Lots of places you could wear a dress like that," Otis said, stepping in. "You'd be surprised at how many parties there are in this town."

"Those who make it in the recording industry know how to party, I imagine," Dill volunteered.

"They're not the only ones," Otis objected. "People get rich doing all kinds of stuff. Of course, people who flip hamburgers can't expect to get nowhere," he added.

Dill jerked away. "Lay off, man."

"Yeah, leave him alone," Nirvana said, putting the dress down.

Otis glanced out the window.

"Teachers can get rich," I piped up. "Jackson owns his

house. Houses in New York City are really expensive."

"That boss of yours ain't rich," said Otis. "He probably scrimped and saved his whole life for that house. Probably a bargain-basement house that the landlord was trying to get rid of. Might have been a condemned building, for all you know. The way you describe that junky old yard of his, I bet that's just what it was."

"How would you know?" I snapped. "You haven't even seen it! You're always trying to put somebody down."

"How about that?" Dill added.

"Don't everybody gang up on me," Otis responded, making his way to the muffin plate. "I don't mean to disrespect that teacher you work for, Haley," he said. "It's just that I have my own dreams."

"What kind of dreams?" Nirvana asked.

He shrugged. "Dreams of a better life." He pointed to the slinky dress with red beads. "My wife is going to have a closet of gowns just as nice as that one. And she's going to have places to wear them. And we won't be walking or taking the subway to get there."

"What kind of car are you going to get?" Dill asked, rubbing his chin. "I want one of those Lincoln Navigators. Throw everything in the back, including the kids."

"I saw a television commercial for a BMW sports car that was definitely me," said Nirvana.

"I won't need a car," I said. "I won't need one, because I'll be living in the city. That's why Jackson doesn't have one."

"People in the city own cars," said Otis. He sat down at the table and propped up his feet. "They own stretches. That's where I'm going to be."

"And how are you going to get there?" Dill challenged. He strutted over to the stack of clothes. "By working in the incense business with that jailbird, Reggie?"

I winced. "Reggie's a jailbird?"

Otis narrowed his eyes at Dill. "Watch your mouth around my sister, man." My brother turned to me. "No, Reggie is not a jailbird. Reggie is my friend." He turned to the window. "Matter of fact, I'm waiting for my friend right now. He was supposed to be across the street a little while ago. He was borrowing a van from somebody to drive our stuff over to the subway stop."

Dill grabbed Nirvana's hand. He gave me a wink. "See you later, chickadee. We've got to be going."

"Wait, Nirvana!" I said, hurrying over to the shopping bag. "My boss gave me some candlestick holders. I thought your grandmother could use them."

"Beautiful!" exclaimed Nirvana, peeking into the bag. "That's nice of you, Haley. Nice of your boss, too," she added, smiling.

"Look what else he gave me!" I dashed across the room and picked Monkey up off the bed.

Nirvana squealed. "A stuffed monkey like the one I used to have!"

"Isn't it a crazy coincidence? And guess what? His name is Monkey, too!"

"Too much!" said Nirvana.

"He's a cute little dude," said Dill, sidling up to see. "Do you still have your stuffed monkey, Nirvana?"

"Somewhere, I suppose."

"Maybe we should save him for our baby," Dill suggested.

Nirvana rolled her eyes. "That's years away," she said firmly.

Dill's face fell. "Can I help it if one of my dreams is to be a good daddy?"

Otis gave him a high sign. "You and me both! Only my kid won't be getting any hand-me-down toys."

Dill flinched, ignoring Otis's upheld hand.

"Hey, I think it stopped raining," I said, running over to the window. I still had on my princess dress. I stuck my head outside. The rain had definitely stopped. Though it was still kind of dreary, the sun was peeking through. Across the street, a crowd was gathering. Something was going on. A police car had pulled up next to a van. A man with his back turned was being frisked. I began to feel shaky.

"Somebody is getting arrested," I announced grimly.

Otis, Dill, and Nirvana rushed over to see. "Aw, man," Otis groaned. He tightened his jaw.

"Who is it?" I asked.

Dill's eyes narrowed. "Looks like Reggie."

Otis made an abrupt about-face. Nirvana grabbed my arm. One of the police officers outside was staring across the street at our building.

"Lock the door, Haley!" Otis cried, dashing out of the apartment.

"Where are you going?" I called in confusion.

"To the bathroom," he yelled, slamming the door. "Don't tell anybody where I am!"

A bolt of fear shot through my body. "What's going on?" I asked Nirvana. Dill pointed outside. A policeman was walking into our building. Across the street, another officer was putting Reggie into the back of the police car. "Is the policeman coming up here?" I asked shrilly.

"Let's get out of here!" Dill said.

"The dress!" Nirvana exclaimed. "Quick, take it off!"

The room began to spin around. Nirvana unzipped me. Then she and Dill yanked the dress off.

"What's happening?" I whispered, stepping out of the swirl of chiffon.

Nirvana took my hand. "Hurry up! We'll go to my place!"

Dill pushed open the door and we burst out into the hall. The policeman was at the bottom of the stairs on his way up. Jerking away from Nirvana, I glanced around wildly. I had heard how these things worked. When there was a crime in the neighborhood, the police picked up all kinds of people as suspects, even if they were innocent. Reggie had done something wrong! So now the police were coming for Otis! My heart thudded. I began to bang on the bathroom door. I had to warn my brother, so that he could get out of there.

"Otis! Hurry up! Run, Otis! Run!" Caught in a well of panic, I wasn't thinking straight. I remember hearing footsteps on the stairs. Then someone was standing behind me. I spun around and found myself face to face with a police officer. He was wearing a gun in his holster and was holding a nightstick.

"Step aside, miss," he said.

I stood in front of the door. "There's nobody in there," I said. My voice sounded hollow. "Just my brother. He's going to the bathroom."

The officer's eyes were sad. "Step aside, please." Dill and Nirvana took my arms and gently pulled me away. The officer knocked on the bathroom door with his nightstick. "Come out with your hands up!" he commanded. My heart stood still. I glanced down at the officer's gun, which was still in his holster.

"Okay," Otis said from behind the door. "I'm coming."

The officer stood aside. The door opened a crack. Otis walked out timidly, holding his hands up.

"Are you Otis Moon?" the officer asked sternly.

My brother nodded.

"Where are your parents?" the policeman asked.

"Not here," Otis muttered.

"Put your hands behind your back," the policeman ordered. Then the officer put handcuffs on him. "You have the right to remain silent...," the policeman began.

I stood there as if in a dream. He was telling Otis his rights, just like in some scene on television. Then, just like that, he was leading my brother away down the stairs. My brother had been arrested!

"Wait!" I cried. "Where are you going with him?"

Otis craned his neck and glanced up at me over his shoulder. "Don't tell Ma," he pleaded.

My legs wobbled. Nirvana hugged me. Dill was leaning against the wall, and Mrs. Brown was standing in her doorway. I didn't know how long she'd been watching.

"I told your mother I couldn't keep up with him," she muttered sorrowfully. "Going out all hours of the day and night."

"It must be a mistake!" I cried.

A different officer came upstairs.

"Where's my brother?" I asked. Tears were streaming out of my eyes.

"We're taking him in," he said, striding into the apartment.

"Why are you going into my apartment?" I whimpered.

Dill touched my arm. "Hush, Haley."

"Yes, let the officer do what he needs to," Mrs. Brown said.

I pulled away and ran down the stairs. Dill and Nirvana followed me.

The crowd on the sidewalk had gotten bigger.

"There he is," Nirvana whispered, pointing to the police car parked across the street. I spied Otis and Reggie seated in the back. Reggie looked a lot older.

"Why are they arresting him?" I cried. I made my way across the street, with Nirvana and Dill on either side of me.

"Reggie was selling hot clothes," Dill explained. "Selling expensive dresses and stuff that he and his friends had ripped off."

"But Otis didn't know that!" I cried. "Otis wouldn't steal anything!"

Venturing through the crowd, I tapped on the window of the police car. Otis turned to me sadly. "Go away!" I could hear him through the glass. "Go home, Haley!"

The officer who had gone up to our apartment came past with an armful of clothes. Dill pulled me out of the way.

"Where are you taking him?" I asked the officer.

"Tell your mother to call the precinct," he directed.

"What are you going to do to him?" I persisted.

"We're going to ask him some questions," the policeman said calmly.

"Come on, Haley," Nirvana said, pulling me gently. I tried to say good-bye to Otis, but he refused to look in my direction. I wandered back across the street and stood with Dill and Nirvana in front of my building. The officer getting the clothes made two more trips. On the last trip, I spotted the white princess dress. Finally, the officer carrying the clothes got into the front of the car with his partner. Then the car took off. Slouched low in the back next to his friend Reggie, my brother didn't look out at me. Dill put an arm around my shoulder.

"Hang in, little chick."

"What are we going to do?" I whispered.

Nirvana held my hand tightly. "You have to tell your mother. Otis will need a lawyer."

"I can't. Otis said not to."

"Maybe he'll beat the rap," Dill said. "Maybe Reggie will take the blame on himself. Otis was probably just following after him."

"Otis is only fifteen," Nirvana said hopefully. "Maybe they'll let him go. Maybe they just took him in to teach him a lesson."

"Maybe the policemen just want to ask Otis some questions," I added, perking up.

Dill smiled. "Maybe in a couple of hours, he'll come sailing right home."

"Come on in here, Haley," Mrs. Brown called down from her window. She'd been watching from her apartment. "Hanging out will just give people something more to talk about."

"I'll be up in a minute." I turned to Nirvana. "Tell me what to do."

"Your mother ought to know," Nirvana advised. "That's her son, after all."

"And the police told you to have her call," Dill reminded me. "You should go and tell her."

"Ma doesn't like me visiting," I said with a swallow.

"Is your ma getting calmed down some?" Dill asked.

"I think so. No telling how she'll take this news about Otis, though." My mouth went dry.

"Will you go to the hospital with me?" I choked, tightening my grip on Nirvana's hand.

"I wish I could. I can't take off from work," she said. "I'll be late as it is, if I don't get moving."

"I can't go, either," said Dill. "Sorry."

I glanced up at Mrs. Brown. "Are you coming inside?" she called down.

"Maybe Grandma could go with you," Nirvana suggested. "You can take a taxi. It's hard for her to walk."

"Or you could call your mother on the telephone," advised Dill. "Break the news to her that way."

"Or wait to see what happens and call her later," Nirvana piped up.

"I could go to the police precinct and wait for Otis," I ventured nervously.

"They might ask you a lot of questions if you show up at the station by yourself," Dill objected.

"About what?" I asked, bewildered. "I didn't steal anything."

"You're thirteen years old and practically living by yourself," Dill reminded me.

"So what?" I said with a shrug.

"They might not like that," Dill advised.

Nirvana and Dill hugged me and walked down the street. I felt completely alone. I sucked in my breath and turned in to the building.

When I got to the top of the stairs, Mrs. Brown was standing in the hallway. "Poor Haley," she said, wagging her head. "That brother of yours is a pure scamp. I feel so sorry for you, child." She clucked her tongue. "I feel so sorry for that poor mother of yours."

"Can we do something for Otis?" I asked weakly.

She pursed her lips. "He and that Reggie got themselves into trouble. Let them get themselves out. As if your poor mother hasn't got enough problems! I'll call her now and break the news."

"No, don't!" I blurted out. "I'll tell her myself, in person. I'm worried about how she'll take it over the telephone."

"Let me know before you leave," Mrs. Brown said, edging into her doorway. "Maybe I can go along with you in a taxicab." She shook her head. "That brother of yours, selling hot clothes. A couple of degenerates—that's what those boys are."

Tears sprang to my eyes. I hung my head. I'd called Otis a degenerate once, too. But I'd been kidding. "He's not a degenerate, Mrs. Brown," I cried. "He's my brother. He's my brother, no matter what he's done!"

"Try to keep calm, Haley," Mrs. Brown said gently.

"Okay," I said, trying to pull myself together.

She went inside and shut her door. The door to my own apartment was still wide open.

"Don't let this be real," I murmured, stepping inside. "Please, let this be a bad dream."

It wasn't a dream, though. My brother had been arrested, and I had to tell my mother about it. And I didn't want to do it alone. I didn't want to wait until visiting hours at three o' clock and go to the hospital with Mrs. Brown, either. But there was someone else I could turn to.

CHAPTER SIX

I stood outside Jackson's house and rang the bell. He opened the door right away. His hair was sticking up as if he'd been napping.

"Come inside," he said in a gentle voice. "Tell me what happened."

I followed him indoors and took a seat in a chair next to the piano. My stomach was churning.

"You sounded upset on the phone," said Jackson. "Has your mother gotten worse?"

"She—she might be pretty soon," I stammered. "There's this problem with my brother. When Ma finds out, I don't know what she'll do."

"What sort of problem does Otis have?" he asked.

I swallowed. "He got arrested."

Jackson looked shocked. "Why? How?"

"It's a long story. But I'm sure he's innocent. My mother has to get him a lawyer. But if I go to the hospital and tell her, she might really go crazy. She's so depressed as it is." I paused to catch a breath. "Ma was just getting better."

Jackson tapped his foot. "When are visiting hours?"

"Not until three o' clock," I said with a moan. "I think I should go now, though. Otis needs Ma's help right away."

"Can you telephone your mother's doctor? He might let you visit earlier."

"I don't know who he is," I said helplessly. "Jackson, I've got to do something quick! The police have my brother."

"We'll go directly to the hospital," he said, picking his keys up off the front table. "If we can't see your mother right away, we'll wait until three."

I bit my lip to keep from crying. "Okay. Thanks."

He laid a hand on my shoulder. "How about a little breather before we leave? I'll get you some orange juice."

I nodded.

He rounded the corner to the kitchen and returned with a glass of juice and a couple of tissues. I blew my nose and drank the juice quickly.

"How do you feel?" he asked.

"Scared." I sighed.

"Did the police come to your apartment?"

I nodded.

"That must have been very scary," he agreed, holding his hand out to me.

"Can you help my brother?" I begged, grasping his hand.

"I'm not sure," said Jackson. "I will do what I can to help you, though," he promised.

We took off for the hospital, which was only a short walk from Jackson's.

"Sorry to ask you to do this," I said, bumping along next to him. "You don't even know my family."

"I don't mind helping out," Jackson assured me.

"My neighbor Mrs. Brown might have gone with me later," I rattled on, "but I didn't want to wait. Besides, I think Mrs. Brown hates Otis."

"I'm glad you called me, Haley," he said, giving my hand a squeeze. "We're friends."

When we got to the hospital, the receptionist at the front desk smiled at me. I smiled back weakly. "Do you think that I can visit a patient?" I asked.

She shook her head. "It's a little early for visiting hours."

"It's an emergency," I explained. "I need to tell my mother something."

"Sorry," the receptionist said. "I can't let you go up without special permission."

"The nurses have met me before," I insisted. "They'll let me come up."

"Maybe we should wait until three o' clock," Jackson said, stepping in. "I'll wait with you down here in the lobby."

"I can't wait," I said, stamping my foot. "Can I talk to somebody in the admitting office?" I begged the receptionist. "My mother works there. She has a friend named Sylvia."

"I'll put you through," the receptionist agreed. She dialed an extension and handed the phone to me. Luckily, Sylvia picked up.

"It's me—Haley," I blurted out. "I really need to see my mother right away, and they won't let me."

"Is there some kind of an emergency?" Sylvia asked in alarm.

"Yes. It's about Otis. Can you ask somebody to let me up? My boss is with me. We're standing at the reception desk."

"Stay right there," said Sylvia. "I'll put you on hold and speak to the nursing station."

My heart skipped a beat. "Sorry for all the fuss," I told the receptionist.

Sylvia got back on. "You can go up, Haley. The nurses gave permission. Let me speak to the receptionist."

"Thanks, Sylvia."

I handed the phone to the receptionist and we hurried toward the elevators.

"Somebody has connections around here," Jackson quipped, striding along next to me. We stepped into the elevator and went up. When the doors slid open on the fourth floor, Ma was standing there. I rushed into her arms. She gave me a hug.

"The nurses told me that you were on your way up," she said softly.

Jackson was standing a little ways behind me.

"This is Jackson, the man I've been working for," I told Ma.

"Pleased to meet you," Ma said. "Thank you for giving Haley a summer job."

"She's a good worker," said Jackson.

Ma motioned me toward a circle of chairs to the left of the elevator. "Let's go over here." Ma and I sat down and Jackson stood close by.

"You aren't crying," I remarked.

"I think that my tear ducts have stopped working,"

she said matter-of-factly. She stared down at her hand. "I've broken a fingernail." I peered at her hand politely.

I took a deep breath. "Ma, something bad happened to Otis." My voice was shaking.

She nodded slowly. "I know. I got a call."

"You know about it?" I exclaimed in surprise. "But you don't seem upset."

"I'm upset," she admitted in a flat voice. "I'm just trying to keep it together."

I looked into her eyes. All the light had gone out of them. Ma wasn't crying the way she had been, but now she seemed like a robot!

"So, is Otis coming home?" I asked hopefully.

"No. I think they're taking him to some facility for juveniles," she reported.

"You're letting them do that!" I cried.

"There will probably be a trial."

"But he's innocent!" I protested.

She sighed. "He confessed," she said helplessly.

"Otis isn't a thief," I insisted.

"He didn't steal the clothes, but he knew they were stolen," Ma explained in a quiet voice. "He and some other boys were selling them at the incense stand. He was mixed up in the whole racket."

"So, that's that?" I choked. "He's guilty, so you're letting them keep him?"

Ma stared at her fingernail. "This thing is hurting," she whispered. "There's not much more I can do for Otis, as long as I'm here," she said, gazing up at me.

"Then come home," I demanded. Jackson stepped in closer.

A few tears glistened in Ma's eyes. "The medication was supposed to make me less depressed, but I didn't count on something like this," she said, standing up. She reached for me. "I love you. I'll call you later."

"If I can do anything to help," Jackson offered, "please let me know, Mrs. Moon."

"Thanks," said Ma. "I'm hoping to be discharged before long. And they're sending a social worker to talk with me." She gave me a distracted look. "So long, sweetheart. I'll let you know when I hear anything." She stared at her hand again, still crying. "Please excuse me. I'll die if I don't take care of this broken fingernail. Maybe one of the nurses can help me."

She turned away from us and walked toward her room. My face got hot.

"Let's go," I said, slamming the elevator button. The elevator came, and we went back down. I kept my eyes straight ahead as we left the building. I pounded my fist into my hand. "I can't believe it," I muttered. "My brother is in jail, and all Ma could do is talk about her broken fingernail! Ma acted as if she doesn't care about Otis at all!" I complained, trudging down the street.

"I'm sure your mother is very upset about your brother," said Jackson.

"She didn't act that way," I spat out. "How can she talk about a broken fingernail at a time like this?"

"Sometimes when the big things seem like too much for us, we focus on the little stuff," Jackson said quietly. "Or maybe your mother was just trying to keep it together, like she said."

"Otis is the one who has to keep it together," I fumed. "He's rotting away in some jail!" My lip quivered. "If only I knew that Otis was all right!"

"Your mother will have some more news later on," Jackson reminded me.

"If she can stop crying long enough to tell me about it," I muttered.

He put his hand on my shoulder. "Let's go back to my

house and have some lunch. You'll feel better if you eat something. Okay?"

I bowed my head. "I'm not hungry."

"I don't want you to be alone," he insisted. "If you like, I can walk you back to Mrs. Brown's."

I shook my head.

"Is there a close relative we can call?"

"No one," I said quietly.

"Then come with me," Jackson said, putting a firm hand on my shoulder.

"What for?" I said with a sigh.

He gave me a little smile. "How about some weeding?"

"I don't feel like it," I moaned. "Besides, I can't tell a weed from a flower."

"There are no flowers in my yard, remember?" he quipped. "All that scrubby stuff along the fence is pure weeds. I know that you're upset. But sometimes it helps to keep busy."

"I don't know..."

Jackson gave me a pat on the back. "I don't have any students today. While you pull the weeds, I'll dig out the dead grass. Don't leave me in the lurch," he cajoled.

"I don't have anything better to do," I mumbled, picking up my pace.

"That's my girl," said Jackson.

In spite of the rain that morning, the weeds seemed to be planted in cement. Jackson gave me a trowel to dig them out. I stabbed the earth and pried up the roots of one. Then I grabbed the weed by its throat and twisted as hard as I could and heaved it out. My knees stung and my hands were sore, but I kept on stabbing and prying and yanking and heaving. "Weeds are so stupid," I murmured angrily.

Jackson worked in silence, clearing the dead lawn with a hoe.

"So, what do you think of my mother?" I muttered, digging my hands into the earth to help out the trowel.

Jackson wiped the sweat from his forehead. "She loves you."

"She's off her rocker," I said snidely. "I still can't believe the thing about the broken fingernail."

Jackson listened patiently.

"If it hadn't been for Ma, Otis might not have gotten into trouble," I vented.

"How do you figure that?" Jackson asked, applying pressure to the hoe.

"If Ma hadn't been in the hospital, Otis wouldn't have had the nerve to stay mixed up with a bad person like Reggie."

"Has your brother been in trouble before?" he asked.

"Not like this," I said. "Ma was beginning to have a hard time controlling him," I admitted. "But Otis wouldn't have done it if Ma had been around."

"I don't think you can automatically blame your mother," said Jackson. "It's hard to figure out why people do the things they do."

"Especially if the people are crazy," I said, stalking over to the shed to get a big garbage bag.

"Your mother couldn't control getting sick," Jackson said quietly. "Mental illness is like any other illness. People don't choose it."

"I know," I said, clenching my jaw. "Ma can't help herself."

Furiously, I began to stuff some weeds into the bag. "So, what's Otis's excuse? Why did he do the crazy stuff he did? Didn't he realize that if he sold stolen clothes, he'd be caught eventually? And to think, I was so proud of him getting a job!"

I tied up the bag of weeds and dragged it to the edge of the yard. Jackson put down the hoe, and we sat under the tree. He offered me some bottled water and I took a swig.

"How do you feel?" Jackson asked.

"I'm not sure," I answered, stretching out on the ground.

"You told me that you were scared," Jackson ventured. "You sound angry, also."

"I feel a lot of things," I murmured. "Inside, I'm totally discomboomerated."

Jackson lifted an eyebrow. "Don't you mean *discombobulated?*"

"Discomboomerated," I insisted, sitting up. "It means upset. It's in my thesaurus. I'm feeling so many things that my whole body is booming."

"Interesting," Jackson said. "I'm not familiar with that word. But I certainly get what you're talking about."

"You probably think it's wrong of me to be mad at Ma and Otis," I challenged. "They're both having such a bad time. But I can't help being angry."

"I'd be angry, too," said Jackson. "Just because you're mad at them doesn't mean you don't love them."

A lump rose in my throat. I forced it down.

"Before she went into the hospital, Ma bought a ton of

groceries. Otis joked that she thought that the world was coming to an end. Maybe she knew that she was going into a bad depression," I said. "Maybe the world *is* ending," I added.

"The world is not ending," Jackson said in a gentle voice. "Lots of good things are in store for you."

I looked into his eyes. He sounded so sure.

He stared out at the yard. "I think our project is shaping up," he said.

"There's no more mess," I admitted, "and almost no weeds."

"I've dug up most of the dead grass," he pointed out. "All I have to do is rake it up."

"It's still not very pretty," I muttered. "Maybe I can make something nice with the fieldstones."

"It's up to you," Jackson said. "You have total artistic freedom."

"I'm not much of an artist," I said. "I like to paint in art class, but lots of other people are better than me."

"I used to be an actor," Jackson said with a little smile. "Lots of people were better than I was, too. But I still enjoyed it."

"You were an actor?" I asked in surprise.

He nodded. "My wife and I had a little theater all our own, before Brielle was born."

"Is that why you had that box of costumes in the shed?"

He nodded.

"What happened to your theater?" I asked curiously.

"We closed it," he replied. "We couldn't make enough money to keep it going."

"Still, it was ambitious of you," I commented.

Jackson chuckled. "You have a way with words. Did anybody ever tell you that?"

I shrugged.

"Maybe you'll be a writer someday," he said.

"What would I write?"

He chuckled. "How about fairy tales? That's what you like reading." He reached over and rubbed my head. "Maybe someday you'll be a great fairy-tale writer and I'll pick up a book in the store and see your name, 'Mahalia Moon.'"

My face flushed. "You think that could happen?"

He nodded.

"Okay," I said, playing along, "I'll write a sequel to 'Hansel and Gretel,' and call it 'Hansel and Gretel Go to the City.' Instead of a wicked witch, I'll create the character of a singing teacher who makes little girls lift heavy stones and pull up weeds all day! I'll even dedicate it to you," I joked.

His eyes sparkled. "Just make sure it has a happy ending."

We got back to work. The weeding was tough, but the more weeding I did, the less discomboomerated I felt. While I finished clearing the edge of the yard, Jackson raked up the dead grass in the middle. Soon all that remained were the tree, the pile of stones, and the bare earth. We stood back and looked at what we'd accomplished. Then Jackson went inside and got a broom.

"Will you do the honors and sweep our dirt yard?"

"I feel kind of silly," I said, taking the broom.

"Sweep the yard," he prodded. "That's what my grandmother did."

I started at the edge and swept carefully. The earth smoothed out. "It *is* peaceful-looking," I murmured, watching the fine lines form in the dirt.

"It's perfect," said Jackson, "just like my childhood."

"Your childhood was perfect?" I asked.

"Far from it," he replied. "But I have some perfect memories, like my grandmother's dirt yard."

"Of course, you can't expect the dirt to stay this way," I pointed out. "The lines will get messed up."

"But we can always sweep it again," he countered cheerfully. "That's the beauty of a having a swept yard. No matter what kind of mess we make, we can always find the broom and straighten things out."

"I hope that your daughter likes it," I said.

Jackson put an arm on my shoulder. "I was wondering about your father, Haley…"

I winced. "What about him?"

"If I were your dad, I'd want to know about Otis's trouble," he remarked in a gentle voice. "I would want to know about your mom being sick, so that I could help out."

"But you're not my dad," I said. "My dad is different. Besides, he's A.U."

"What's that mean?" asked Jackson.

"Address Unknown," I said, striding toward the tree. "That's what I write on all my school forms where they ask for the father's address."

"If you'd like, we can try to find him," offered Jackson.

"I don't think so," I said, turning away. "He was pretty mean to Ma," I confided. "I saw some bad things. So did Otis. Ma had to get an order of protection so he wouldn't come and bother her. "

"I'm sorry," he said quietly.

I sighed. "To tell the truth, it's kind of confusing. Even though Dad was mean to Ma, he was often nice to me. I loved it when he read to me. It hurts to think about, so I try not to."

"I didn't mean to pry," said Jackson.

I gave him a little smile. "That's okay." I had never met anyone as kind as Jackson! "You and Brielle are lucky," I said wistfully.

"Nobody's life is perfect," Jackson commented. He stood up taller. "Ready to go home now?"

I nodded. "Ma might be calling with some news about Otis. And I never told Mrs. Brown where I was going. She offered to go with me to the hospital during visiting hours."

"Let's hurry, then," Jackson said. He pressed a safety lock on the glass doors and shut them.

"You don't have to walk me home," I told him.

"I know," he said, edging toward the front of the house. "But I want to make sure that you're safe."

We walked the short distance to my building in comfortable silence.

"This is us," I said, stopping in front of the stoop.

"I love the architecture," he commented.

"Thanks. So do I. A long time ago, it was a hotel." I pointed up at our windows. "See that yellow thing in the tiniest window on the second floor? That's our cookie jar. Ma once told me that if I ever got lost, I could look for the cookie jar in that window and find my way home. Just look for the Cookie Jar Hotel."

He smiled. "Your cookie jar is kind of a beacon."

"Sometimes I think of the fire escape as a balcony," I confided. "Ma got mad at me once because I went out there in my pajamas."

He chuckled.

"Sometimes I imagine that ladies are strolling up there on the fire escape," I said softly.

"What do the ladies look like?" he mused.

"Brown skin, lacy white dresses, pink parasols. They're holding china cups," I confided dreamily.

He smiled. "Quite an imagination you've got there."

"Thanks for everything," I said, turning in toward the building. "See you on Monday!"

Jackson waved and took a step down the sidewalk. A familiar voice floated down to the street.

"Thought I heard you, Mahalia Moon!" Mrs. Brown said, popping her head out her window. "Where have you been?"

I looked up. "Visiting Ma," I called. "I couldn't wait. I'm sorry if I worried you. After I saw Ma, I went to work." I motioned to Jackson. "This is my boss."

Jackson nodded, and Mrs. Brown nodded politely.

"Did Ma call?" I asked Mrs. Brown.

She shook her head. "I tried to call her, but there wasn't any answer. Come on in. Nirvana and Dill are waiting for you over in your apartment."

Jackson gave me a wink and turned away for the second time. "Thanks for the good job you did today. Call me if you need me."

"I will," I promised. "Thanks again."

I went inside and climbed the stairs. Nirvana was peeking out my door.

"Come on in!" she said. "We have a surprise." She opened the door wider to reveal a room filled with lovely, flickering candles stuck in Mrs. Brown's new candlestick holders. The table was set with three plates. Dill was sitting in Otis's spot with a grin on his face.

"I thought you'd never get here," he complained. "I'm starving."

"Grandma cleaned your apartment," Nirvana explained excitedly. "And Dill and I put out the dishes and silverware." She pointed to two serving bowls on the table. "Grandma made some spaghetti and meatballs and green salad!"

"We didn't want you to eat by yourself," Dill explained.

"This is great," I said, throwing my arms around Nirvana. Then I rushed to the sink and washed my hands. "I really like the candles!"

Nirvana cleared her throat. "Dill went out and bought them. We kind of have to have them," she added quietly.

"Why? It's not dark yet," I remarked, sitting down at the table. I gave her a playful look. "Oh, I get it! You lit them to be romantic."

"The man from the electric company came today," Mrs. Brown announced, appearing in the doorway.

"He cut off your lights," Nirvana explained.

Dill reached for the spaghetti. "We don't need electricity. We've got candles."

"Let's eat," Nirvana encouraged, serving my plate. "We can worry about the electric bill later."

"Though I don't know where we'll get the money from," said Mrs. Brown.

I let out a groan and remembered the bills that Ma had

buried beneath the knives in the silverware drawer. I hadn't bothered to check them out. "What else can go wrong?" I said with a sigh.

"I might be able to lend you some money, Haley," Dill offered, touching my hand.

"That's okay," I said, trying to be brave. "I have the money I've made from my job put away in the cookie jar. I was saving it for a rainy day, after all."

"And this is the rainy day!" Mrs. Brown said enthusiastically. "Nirvana will take you over to the electric company to pay the bill on her day off."

Nirvana patted me on the back. "Don't worry, Haley. You've got us. We'll get you through."

"Thanks," I said.

Mrs. Brown turned away. "You children eat up, now. I'll see you later."

I was sitting down to the table when the telephone rang. I jumped up to answer it. It was Ma.

"How are you, sweetheart?"

"Fine. What about Otis?"

"He's okay. I spoke with him. He's in a juvenile facility until his trial date, just like I expected. Maybe he could have waited at home, if I hadn't been in the hospital," she added quietly.

My heart clutched. "How long are they going to keep him?"

"We're not sure," said Ma. "We have to take one day at a time. The social worker came after you left today. A nice lady named Terry. She'll probably come to see you, too. Try not to worry. If it's the last thing I do, I'm going to get well."

"You sound better," I said hopefully.

"The doctor is still adjusting the dosage of my medication," she murmured. "This thing with Otis has kind of thrown me." She paused.

"Be cooperative, Haley."

"Okay," I promised. "Ma?"

"Yes?"

"Get well. Please."

"I'm working on it...," she said wearily.

"Is everything all right?" Nirvana called out.

"They've put Otis in a juvenile facility," I told her after I hung up. "Ma can't do anything about it." All the panicky feelings I'd had that morning rushed back suddenly. I sat down at the table again and began jiggling my foot.

"Things will get better, Haley," said Dill.

"Eat your dinner," encouraged Nirvana.

I picked at my spaghetti, trying hard not to cry. "I'll be all right," I told them.

"Whatever happens, Grandma and I are right next door," Nirvana assured me.

Dill reached for my hand. "I'm here for you, too. We're sticking like glue, until your mother gets better."

Nirvana squeezed my shoulder. "You're our little sister, Haley."

But the world didn't see it that way.

CHAPTER SEVEN

Nirvana slept over with me that night. She started out on Otis's couch bed, but when she heard me tossing and turning, she got up in the dark and gave me a hug.

"Poor Haley, I'm sorry things are going so badly for your family."

"Things will get better," I said quietly.

"Would you like for me to sleep in your bed with you?" she asked, tugging on the edge of my sheet.

"Okay," I said, perking up. "You take the top of the bed and I'll take the bottom. We'll sleep head to feet."

"Good plan," said Nirvana. She climbed in. I scrunched my body over to make room for her.

"Did you ever know anybody in jail?" I asked.

"No," she replied. "But I've heard it can be rough."

"What do you mean by that?" I asked fearfully.

"I've heard that you meet up with a lot of rough customers inside," she said quietly. "But don't worry. Otis is smart. He'll stay away from the wrong people."

"He wasn't smart enough to stay away from Reggie," I murmured.

"Try to get your mind off it," Nirvana suggested. "Try to go to sleep."

I sighed. We were quiet for a minute. I stared up at the ceiling.

"Pretty dark in here tonight, huh?" I whispered.

She grunted softly.

"How soon do you think they can turn the lights back on?" I asked.

"They're usually pretty quick to take care of things after you pay up," she answered in a sleepy voice. "The same thing happened to me and Grandma once." She rolled over and faced the wall. "Night, Haley. Sleep tight. Don't worry." In a couple of minutes, I heard her snoring.

I squinted out into the room. A shiver went through me. When I was little, I had never been afraid of scary stories, but I had been afraid of the dark. The fact that I wouldn't be able to turn on the lamp, if I suddenly needed to, freaked me out. It reminded me of the old days when I was afraid of the boogeyman. There was a tiny bit of light in the room, filtering in from the streetlamp, but somehow that made things even eerier. The closet door was open, and I was sure that someone was there. I closed my eyes tight. But what I imagined when my eyes were shut was even scarier. I saw Otis carrying a severed head! Blood was dripping every-where, and the blood drops were calling, "Haley! Haley!"

I jerked my eyes open and sat up in bed. Nirvana was still sleeping soundly. I peered across the room once more. Some-one was definitely hiding in the closet! I held my breath. I could hear a slight tapping sound. Maybe a robber had broken in while I had been gone that day, I thought. The person was just waiting for me to go to sleep before jumping out. When I woke up, all our stuff would be stolen. Or maybe the robber had already stolen our stuff and left! Working up my nerve, I crept out of bed and scurried across the room. I heard the slight tapping again. Maybe this time there was a real rat in the oven, I thought, shrinking away from the stove. I stared at the clown cookie jar above the sink. My money had been in-side it! I took off the top and touched the wad of dollar bills. My stash was still safe. Relieved, I put the top back on the jar and felt for a glass on the counter. I turned on the water and filled the glass. I drank a few sips. The clown cookie jar stared at me. I had always liked its cheerful smile, but now the clown seemed to be mean and leering. I swallowed, unable to tear my eyes away.

I leaned toward the window. A tiny breeze was coming in. The coolness stroked my cheek. The window shade was partway up. It stirred slightly. The plastic knob at the end of the pull cord gently knocked on the screen, creating the tapping noise that I'd heard.

I thought about Otis. He must have been lonely. I wondered what kind of beds they had in the juvenile facility. I was pretty sure there were no pullout couches like the one that Otis was used to sleeping on. Maybe the "juveniles" had to sleep on hard cots for punishment. Or even worse, no beds at all! My imagination began to run wild. I saw Otis stretched out on a cold, dank floor. For dinner he might have had only bread and water. He'd be so hungry that he would try to break out. I imagined Otis climbing out a tiny window and up onto a roof. On the street below was Reggie, who'd also made an escape. Instead of the van that Reggie had borrowed, there was a stretch limo. My brother would leap off the roof and jump into the car. He and Reggie would roar away. Then, from out of nowhere, a police car would chase them. Otis and Reggie would be in more trouble than ever when they got caught.

I shook my head to snap out of it. What I had imagined

was ludicrous. They had to have real beds in a juvenile facility. It was probably a law. And how on earth could Reggie come up with a stretch limo that fast? And if Otis tried jumping off a roof, he would only get hurt. I should have laughed at myself—I was being so ridiculous. But a tear rolled out of my eye instead. Who knew when I would see my brother again?

I tiptoed across the room to look once more at the "robber" in the closet. It was only Ma's dress, the soft blue one that she looked so lovely in. On the floor next to our pile of shoes was my basketball. I hadn't tried it yet.

I nestled down in bed next to Nirvana's feet. I carefully touched one of her toes. Ma had paid lots of money for Otis's sneakers. Since Nirvana worked at a sneaker store, she probably got a break on hers. My thoughts began to get scrambled. I imagined Otis taking his shoes off in prison. There would be all kinds of criminals around going to bed, too. If Otis wasn't careful, somebody might steal his sneakers from him. Ma would be more upset than ever if Otis came home without his shoes....

The next thing I knew, it was morning. The sun was shining brightly and Nirvana was gone. She'd left a note on the table.

Haley,
Had to take Grandma to church.
Love,
Nirvana.

I opened the door and made a beeline for the bathroom. I brushed my teeth and washed my face. When I got back to the apartment, there was a strange woman standing in the middle of the room.

"Who are you?" I demanded.

She smiled and stuck out her hand. "I didn't mean to startle you. The door was wide open."

"Get out," I choked, backing away. "This is my apartment."

She nodded. "You're Mahalia Moon, aren't you? I'm Terry Soriano, a social worker. Your mother said she'd tell you I was coming."

I went inside, but left the door open a crack. "Sorry," I yelled, scooting across the room. "I didn't know who you were."

"That's okay. May I sit down?"

"Okay." I grabbed my jeans and T-shirt off the floor and held them in front of me.

"Looks like you had company for dinner last night," she commented, eyeing the spaghetti dishes in the sink. She smiled. "Looks like it was good."

"My friend Nirvana and her boyfriend, Dill," I said, leaning against the counter. "Nirvana's grandmother made dinner for us. I was going to clean up this morning," I added apologetically.

"Is Nirvana's grandmother Mrs. Brown?" she asked.

I nodded. "How do you know Mrs. Brown?"

"Your mother told me about her. Does she make breakfast for you as well?"

"Not really," I said, leaning against the counter. "For breakfast I usually grab something at Rivera's. They have the greatest doughnuts. Have you been there?"

"I tried them once," she said. "Kind of sugary. I'm on a diet."

I eyed her suspiciously. I'd never heard anyone say anything bad about Rivera's doughnuts!

She took a notebook out of her bag and wrote something down.

"What are you writing?" I asked, still clutching my clothes. You'd think that she'd have given me some privacy!

"I want to make sure you're well taken care of," she said. She gave me a smile that I was sure was phony.

"My mother does that," I said shrilly.

"I'm here to help your mother," said Terry. She smiled again. "She asked me to, yesterday at the hospital."

I swallowed. "Do you know about Otis?"

Terry nodded. "I'm so sorry about what happened to him. You must be upset."

"Not really," I lied. "He'll get out. He's innocent."

Terry looked at me thoughtfully.

"Did you see him?" I asked.

"I did," she replied. "He's sorry for what he's done."

"Did he tell you that?" I asked in surprise.

"Yes. He also told your mother."

"Can I speak with him, too?" I asked eagerly.

"Not unless he wants you to," she said in a quiet voice.

"But he will want to speak with me," I pressed. "I'm his sister."

"I'm not sure that he wants to speak to anybody but your mom at the moment," she said hesitantly.

I frowned. "I don't like standing here in my pajamas," I blurted out angrily. "I'm going into the closet to change."

"Of course," Terry said, standing up. "I should have

given you a moment to get dressed. It was thoughtless of me."

"Forget it," I said, turning in to the closet with my jeans.

"Mind if I peek in the refrigerator?" she called over her shoulder.

"Go ahead," I called back. "Help yourself, if you're hungry. My mother bought tons of groceries before she went into the hospital. Of course, none of us is on a diet," I murmured sarcastically.

When I came out of the closet, Terry was holding a milk carton. "Mind if I throw this away?" she asked. "It's spoiled."

I shrugged. "Too bad. Probably because there's no electricity. I hope everything else didn't spoil."

Terry poured the milk into the sink and tossed out the carton. "How long have you been without electricity?" she asked, picking up her notebook again.

"Only one night. I don't mind, really. Nirvana said she'd sleep over so that I won't be scared. Nirvana used to be my baby-sitter."

"Did her friend Dill sleep over, too?" she asked.

"Of course not!" I said with a nervous laugh. "Are you crazy? Mrs. Brown would kill her! Are you trying to say something nasty about my friends?"

"No, certainly not," said Terry.

"It sounded that way to me," I countered stubbornly.

"I'm sorry," said Terry. "I'm sure Nirvana and Dill are great people. You probably feel very close to the Browns."

"I feel close to Nirvana," I said hesitantly, "but I don't always feel close to Mrs. Brown," I confessed. "She called Otis a degenerate. I didn't like that."

"Would you consider sleeping over at her house?" Terry asked.

"I'd hate it," I answered. "She has cats. Cats give me hives. I'm allergic to them."

"Your mom mentioned that," Terry said thoughtfully. "Why don't we go next door? I'd like to meet Mrs. Brown."

"She's at church," I explained. "Nirvana went with her."

"So you're all alone?"

"What does it look like?" I snapped. I was getting tired of all her questions and the way she was staring at me, as if I were someone to feel sorry for. "I'm really okay here by myself," I assured her. "Otis and I were living alone before he left. We did just fine."

"Children shouldn't be alone, Haley," she said.

I looked her in the eye. "I'm not a child."

"Yes, you are," she said.

A feeling of dread came over me. Something awful was about to happen! "I won't be alone…when—when Ma comes home," I stammered. "I'm not alone now. I have neighbors."

"I don't think that's quite enough," Terry said. "I hope you don't find it too upsetting," she continued, "but while she's in the hospital, your mother and I would like for you to live somewhere else."

For a moment, the breath was knocked out of me. "Where?" I cried. "I don't understand! This is my apartment! You're not going to take me away!" I said, rushing for the telephone. "My mother won't let you!" I grabbed the phone and punched in Ma's number. Luckily, she picked up right away.

"Ma!"

"Good morning, Haley."

"There's a social worker here who wants to take me someplace!" I glanced at Terry and backed away. I hated her! "You didn't tell her to do that, did you?"

"Is her name Terry Soriano?" Ma asked quietly.

"Yeah, but—"

"Put her on," Ma interrupted.

I dropped the phone. I was doomed. "She wants to speak with you."

Terry gave me a little smile and picked up the phone.

I stood there listening with a scowl on my face.

"Hello, Mrs. Moon? Your lights have been cut off and your neighbor is nowhere to be found. I have a spot for Haley. I can take her with me right now."

"You're not taking me anywhere!" I shouted.

"Your daughter is very upset," Terry continued, talking to Ma. "It's only natural." She paused.

"What is Ma saying?" I cried.

"Why don't you speak with her yourself?" Terry suggested in a gentle voice. I took a few steps forward, and she handed me the telephone.

"Ma?" My heart was beating a mile a minute.

"Please cooperate, Haley."

I gasped. "You mean I have to go with her? Leave our apartment?"

"It will only be for a little while, until I get out of here," Ma said. I could hear that she was already crying.

"But what if Otis comes home?" I argued. "I won't be here."

"Do as I say, Haley," she pleaded. "You don't have a choice."

"I would if you would come home."

"This is for your own safety, darling."

"Mrs. Brown is taking care of—"

"I have to trust the social worker," said Ma. "Get hold of yourself."

"Where is she going to take me?"

"A group boarding home," Ma explained. "It's only temporary."

"But I didn't do anything!" I argued. "Otis is the one who stole the clothes!"

"Calm down, Haley," Ma said firmly. "This isn't because you did anything wrong. This is for your protection."

Terry stepped in closer. "Why don't you hang up now, Haley? You can call your mother later on, when you're settled."

"I don't want to get settled," I said with an angry sob.

"Haley?" Ma's voice floated over the telephone wire. "You can do this. You're brave."

I slammed down the phone. "I don't care what she says. I'm not going."

Terry gazed into my face. She looked truly sorry. "I know how upsetting this is. You'll be able to come back home when your mother gets well. You can even make trips here before then. A social worker will come with you. I know you'll want to check in or pick up more of your things."

I slumped down at the table and hid my face.

"I'll give you a moment to pull yourself together," she said. "Then we'll pack some clothes. Don't forget that your mother agrees that this is a good plan. There are other kids in the boarding home."

"What kind of home is it?" I sniffed, lifting my head. I couldn't believe it was happening! First Otis, then me! "How far away is it?" I whimpered.

"It's a nice apartment in a building something like your own," she explained. "It's not far away at all. You'll still be in your own neighborhood." She patted my hand. "Hopefully, it'll only be for a little while. Come now, get ready. Would you like for me to pack your stuff?"

I jerked up from the table. "Please don't. I'll do it myself."

Ma had taken the suitcase, so I packed my things in my box. Once upon a time, I had imagined that Ma had slid into a well, but now I was the one sliding down. I was slipping on all the feelings I had inside. One minute I felt like crying, and the next minute I felt like hitting Terry over the head and breaking the walls down. I knew I

147

should cooperate to please Ma, but I felt like locking myself in the closet and never coming back out. I slammed my *Grimms'* into the box with my pajamas. I rolled up Grandma Dora's earrings in one of my socks. While Terry wrote something on a piece of paper from her notebook, I got my money out of the cookie jar and shoved it into my wallet. It was hard to think what to take; I wouldn't be gone long, I told myself. I couldn't be! Overalls, shirt, Monkey, the snake. I grabbed Otis's toothbrush, forgetting my own. I also took my thesaurus, though a word had not yet been invented for the way that I felt.

I sat down on my bed, holding the box.

"Ready?" asked Terry.

"What about Nirvana and Mrs. Brown?" I choked. "They'll be worried about me."

"I'll slip a note under their door and telephone Mrs. Brown later," she promised. "Let's go."

I took a last look at my unmade bed, then at Ma's bed and at Otis's couch, at the tub, the table, and the crack in the ceiling. I didn't cry. My tears were blocked up inside of me, because there were too many to let out.

Terry had told the truth. The boarding home wasn't far

away, located in a dull brown building. The apartment, which was on the first floor, was much larger than ours, but everything was a yellow that reminded me of mucus. Yellow curtains hung at the window. On the table was a yellow tablecloth, and on the beds were yellow spreads. The apartment had three rooms: a big kitchen with a table and chairs, and two bedrooms. I would be sharing a bedroom with two other girls, Yvonne and Maria, both of whom seemed younger than me. There was a woman, too, named Angela. When Terry introduced me to the three of them, I kept my eyes glued to the floor. Terry led me into the bedroom with my things, and the others followed us.

"In a while we're going to the park for a softball game," Yvonne, the littler girl, said. I guessed that she was about eight. "Do you like softball?"

I lay down on my bed and turned away. "Softball is for dorks," I breathed softly.

"Did you say something?" asked Maria. She was chubby and the older of the two. I kept my lips glued.

"What's *her* problem?" Maria asked Terry.

"Mahalia is tired," said Terry. "Maybe we should let her rest for a while."

"Yes, we'll leave you alone for a bit," Angela said quietly. Then the four of them trailed away.

I was tired, but I didn't shut my eyes. How could Ma think this was better than my staying by myself or even sleeping at Mrs. Brown's? Living in an apartment with yellow stuff and total strangers?

After about fifteen minutes or so, Angela and Terry came back into the room. Unlike Terry, who wore her gray hair in a bun, Angela wore her black hair in a long braid. She touched me softly on the back. "Would you like a snack? We've got chips and all kinds of good stuff."

"I don't want a snack," I muttered, jerking away.

"How long will she be here?" Angela asked Terry.

"We're not sure," replied Terry.

I turned my head and glared. "I don't like it when people talk about me as if I weren't even here," I said.

"Sorry," said Angela. "Would you like us to leave you alone again?"

"Yes," I snapped.

The two women tiptoed out. The apartment was deadly quiet. I guessed they'd decided to give me the silent treatment. I lay on my bed for what seemed like a hundred hours, trying not to be scared. I had never lived away from home.

That's one reason Ma had always wanted me to go to camp, so that I could have the experience.

Angela came back into the room, this time by herself. She smiled, but, thankfully, kept her distance. I didn't like my back being touched by a stranger.

"Ready to come out now?" she asked. "Rayelle has taken the other girls for ice cream."

"I thought they were going to play softball," I said, peering up at her.

She nodded. "Then after that, they were going for ice cream."

I turned my face to the wall and muffled my mouth with my fist. "Who's this Rayelle person?" I grumbled.

Angela leaned closer, trying to understand me.

"Who is Rayelle?" I demanded in a louder voice.

"She's the other woman who works here," Angela explained. "Sometimes we have shifts together, and at other times we're here alone with the girls." I peeked at her face. Her eyes were kind.

"We like to think of ourselves as temporary mothers," she told me.

Panic rose in my chest. I already had a mother!

"Where's Terry?" I asked crossly.

"Terry had to leave," said Angela. "She'll be back tomorrow to check on you."

"Does she live here?" I asked.

"No," said Angela. She perched on the edge of the bed. "I know it must be confusing for you—all these new people."

"I don't care," I said with a shrug.

"Why don't you get up and stretch your legs?" she cajoled. "You'll feel better if you do."

I dragged myself out of bed and followed her into the kitchen. One of my legs had actually fallen asleep. I hopped around in front of the refrigerator. Yellow smiley faces were pasted all over it. "The kids in this place must come from sick homes," I sniped.

"Why do you think that?" asked Angela.

"Because they're happy to be here," I said.

"You're not, are you?"

"No, why should I be? I come from a great family." A pain shot through my chest. "We just happen to be going through a rough spot. My brother got into trouble, but he's not a bad guy. My mother is in the hospital, but any day she'll be well."

"I'm sure she will," Angela said quietly. "I made some

egg salad," she said. "Would you like a sandwich?" She plopped the egg salad onto some bread.

"I don't eat egg salad. It smells like farts." I stared at the table. "Do you know what kinds of lunches they serve in jail?"

"I think they try to serve balanced meals," Angela replied kindly. She poured me a glass of water. "Drink this."

"I'm not thirsty." I clamped my mouth and rolled my eyes.

"You'll get dehydrated," she persisted, "especially in this hot weather."

"No."

"So you refuse to eat or drink, then?"

"Yes," I replied in defiance. "I'm on a hunger strike, and that includes water."

"And what must I do in order for you to end the strike?" Angela asked in a serious tone.

"Let me out of here."

"Sorry," said Angela. "We can't do that."

"Then at least don't bother me," I said, turning toward the room where my bed was.

Yvonne and Maria burst into the apartment, giggling and clutching ice cream cones. I looked at them over my shoulder. An older woman in a dress covered with an autumn-leaf design was with them.

"This is Rayelle," Angela said.

The leaf-dress woman smiled at me. "Hello, Mahalia."

"Hi," I grunted, walking away.

"How is she?" I heard Rayelle ask.

"Pretty irritable," Angela replied, talking about me as if I weren't there.

"Want a lick of ice cream?" Yvonne asked, racing after me.

"Why would I want to eat that melted mess?" I snarled. "Look, it's dripping all down your arms. You're really a slob! Why don't you smear some egg salad on top of it?"

"That's not nice!" Yvonne whined, following me into the bedroom. "Did you hear what she said to me?" she called to Maria with a pout.

"Better watch your mouth," Maria said, strutting into the room.

"Watch yours," I shot back, "or I'll get my brother to beat you up. He's a big-time crook." Both Maria and Yvonne backed off. I sat down on my bed.

Angela came into the room. "Would you like to speak with your mom?" she asked, sitting down next to me. "We could call her."

"No, thanks," I said. "She'll only be crying."

I lay down and curled up into a ball. When Angela left, I reached down into my box and pulled out Monkey. I stared at the wall while life in the apartment went on. Sounds of laughter came from the kitchen. I could hear Yvonne and Maria playing games. When I heard the clanging of pots and pans and the clatter of dishes, I knew it was dinnertime. My stomach rumbled, but I felt too upset to eat. Later on, Yvonne and Maria came into the bedroom and changed into their pajamas. Finally, I heard someone walking toward my bed.

"Time for lights-out. Don't you want to change?" It didn't sound like Angela, but I refused to look.

I pretended to be asleep, but I wasn't. My heart ached. I missed Otis. And even though Ma had let them take me away, I missed her more than ever. I heard her voice in my ear. *Be cooperative, Haley.* I barely slept.

When morning came, I popped up and quietly crept into the kitchen. Angela was there, packing lunches.

"Good morning," she said. "Feel any better?"

"A little," I said politely. I looked down at my clothes. "I guess I got wrinkled."

"Would you like to take a shower?" she asked. "There's a

lock on the bathroom door. You can shower and change in private in there."

"Maybe later," I said hesitantly.

She offered me a glass of orange juice. I took a gulp. She offered me a piece of toast and I gobbled it down.

"Rayelle said your mother called last night while you were asleep," Angela told me. "Your mom didn't want you to be awakened."

My heart skipped a beat. I had missed Ma's call!

"But I wasn't asleep," I protested. "Did you speak to her?"

She shook her head. "I had gone home already," Angela explained. "Rayelle spent the night here."

"Where is Rayelle now?" I asked curiously.

"She went home at six." She went back to making lunches.

I began to pace. It was too early to call Ma at the hospital. *She probably just wanted to make sure I was being cooperative*, I thought. I wrinkled my nose at the smiley faces on the refrigerator. I glanced at Angela.

"Every time I see you, you're making a sandwich," I grumbled.

"Do you like jelly with your peanut butter?" she inquired.

"Sure," I muttered. "But you don't have to make me lunch."

"Oh, you'll need a lunch at the pool," said Angela.

"What pool?"

"The neighborhood pool. There's a program there. Kind of like a day camp. Yvonne and Maria love it. You'll go there right after your physical."

I blinked. "Physical?"

"Terry is going to take you to the clinic for a physical and then drop you off at the pool."

"But I don't need a physical."

"Don't worry," she said, "no needles, just a routine checkup. It's policy."

"I can't go," I said.

"Why not?"

"I have a job," I explained. "I have to go to work."

"Nobody said anything about a job," Angela said.

"Well, I have one," I insisted, "and it's very important."

"I can't permit you to go," said Angela.

"My boss is depending on me," I said hotly.

"Sorry," she said.

I folded my arms across my chest. "I'm going, whether you like it or not."

"Mind your attitude," Angela said crisply. "You can't go anywhere without our permission." She threw some apples into the bags. "Where is this job, anyway?"

"In Queens," I lied, narrowing my eyes. If she wasn't going to let me go, what business was it of hers?

"That's out of the question, then," Angela said, glancing at the clock. "Have another piece of toast. I have to wake up Yvonne and Maria." She turned her back and went into the bedroom. I opened the front door and walked out.

CHAPTER EIGHT

I bolted out of the apartment building and ran as fast as I could. The only thing I could do was run away. How could I stay with a dictator like Angela, who didn't care if my life got wrecked? Didn't she understand that everything I had, had been taken away? Ma, Otis, my apartment—and now she'd taken my job! If there was nothing left in my life, what was the point of staying in some boarding home? So that I could go swimming every day with a bunch of little brats? I was so mad I could hardly see straight. I ducked into a subway station. I needed a place to think. But it was so hot underground, I felt as if I might faint. Impulsively, I reached into my pocket for some change, bought a token at the booth, and bumped through the turnstile. A whistle blared, warning of the approaching train. A man standing next to me inched forward. If I got on the train, too, where would it take me? Only a few stops away was Port Authority, the big bus terminal. Buses left from the station for places all over the country. The subway screeched to a halt, and I rushed forward with the crowd as the doors yawned open and people pushed their way in or out of the train. Wiggling my way through, I stepped into the train and found a pole to hold on to. People squeezed in close to me on either side. I found it hard to breathe as we traveled toward 42nd Street. Lots of other people were getting off there, too. I let myself be pushed along by the crowd. Then I was out again, standing on the platform.

I followed the signs to the bus terminal. On the first floor of the terminal, there was a newsstand and a coffee shop and lots of lines for tickets and people everywhere! I even saw the man with no legs, riding around on a low platform. He was the same man that I'd seen crossing in front of Rivera's. I waited for him to smile at me, but he didn't look up. He just scooted himself along.

I selected a line to stand in. I wasn't quite sure where I would go. I figured I might go as far as my money would take me. I smoothed my hair back with my hand and waited my turn. Then I was face to face with a woman behind the counter. She stared at me.

"May I help you?"

"How much does one ticket cost?" I asked timidly.

"A ticket to where?"

I took a deep breath. "To Disney World," I blurted out.

"Orlando, Florida? I'll check," she said. She glanced over my shoulder and nodded. A policeman stood near the door. I stood up tall. I was sure that there wasn't a law against going to Disney World, but I began to feel scared that I might be arrested. I turned back to the counter. The woman was staring at me with a cross look on her face.

"Miss?"

"Yes. How much?"

"I just told you the price," she said in an exasperated voice. "Do you want the ticket or not?"

I glanced back over my shoulder. The policeman was gone.

I felt dizzy. I grabbed on to the counter to steady myself.

"Do you want the ticket or not?" the woman repeated angrily.

My shoulders drooped. "No thanks." I chickened out. Besides, Disney World was a trip Ma wanted the three of us to take together someday. It wouldn't have been the same without her and Otis along. I stepped out of line and slowly walked away. I wiped away a tear of frustration as my feet led me out of the bus terminal to the downtown subway station. Ma was depending on me to be cooperative. Not only that—

if I ran away, I might never find out what happened to Otis. But there was something I had to do before I went back to that mucus-colored apartment with all its smiley faces. I had made a promise. I had a job to do. I bought another token. Jackson's house would be only a short ride away. A train came and I hopped in. Soon I was running again, up the stairs and into the sunlit street.

When I arrived at Jackson's, the second-story blinds were still drawn. I found my way to the backyard stone pile and paused to rest, pressing my back into its cool, sharp edges. *These stones must have seen so much,* I thought, *in this spot for hundreds of years, ever since a farmer dug them up. The whole world has changed around them.*

I turned and lifted a big flat one from the top of the pile and set it in the middle of the yard. The glass doors flung open and Jackson walked out.

"You're here earlier than usual," he said. "How was the weekend?"

"Okay," I replied, keeping my eyes fixed on the ground.

"You seem kind of low," Jackson said with concern. "How is Otis? Did something else happen?"

"I missed Ma's call last night. I guess he's same-old,

same-old," I mumbled. I swallowed hard and fixed my eyes on the back of the yard. "I'm starting with the stones today."

"I can't wait to see what you come up with," he said in a thoughtful way. I could feel him staring at me. "Are you sure you're okay?"

"Fine," I replied, trying to sound cheerful. The front doorbell rang. "Right on time," Jackson observed, glancing at his watch. "I'm teaching straight through until twelve. See you!" He went inside, closing the glass doors behind him.

A moment later, I heard sounds of the piano and the off-key voice of a boy struggling with scales. I bent down in front of the pile of stones and hurriedly began to sort through them, trying not to think about the trouble I'd be in when I went back to the boarding home.

I'd never seen so many stones in my life! They were all shapes and sizes. Some were flat and others were nearly round; some had smooth edges and others were jagged. Three at the very bottom were so huge they could almost have been miniature boulders. I'd never be able to move those, no matter how strong I thought I was. I began to play around with the smallest ones. They reminded me of odd-shaped loaves of bread. I began to line them up, side by side and touching, along the edge of the yard where the weeds had once been....

When I was finished, there was a stone border on three sides! On the fourth side, I created a path with smaller stones lining either side of it. The path started from the tree and led up to the glass doors.

I'd used up lots of stones, but there were still some left. I wiped my face with the tail of my shirt. I'd been working so hard that I'd lost track of time, and the boy who had been singing was long gone. Shari, my favorite soprano, was singing now, a very fast song in a foreign language.

My eyes fell on the flat rock I'd placed in the center of the yard earlier. I made a dash to the pile and plucked off another one, also flat, but a wee bit smaller. I hoisted it back to the center of the yard and placed it on top of the stone on the ground. I made a few more trips like that and kept on stacking. In no time, I had a sculpture. I stepped back to look at it. I'd built a stone person!

I hastily set about building other stone people all over the yard: a tall one next to the tree, a short one by the door, three standing side by side right near the side gate. I almost laughed out loud. There were so many stone people in the yard, it was almost too crowded. Jackson came out, surprising me.

"A sculpture garden!" he cried. "How did you think of that?"

"Haven't you ever built a snowman?" I said.

"What's that have to do with it?" said Jackson.

I smiled. "Instead of snowmen, these are *stone*men. I just picked up some stones and kept stacking."

"I get it," he said with a chuckle. "But it also reminds me of a miniature Stonehenge!"

"What's that?"

"Assemblages of gigantic rocks, set up by prehistoric people in England."

"Wow! I didn't know I was doing all that!" I said, flushing.

"Seriously, I love it," he said, touching one of the sculptures. "I can't believe how much you've done in just one morning. The whole stone pile is gone."

"All except for those three huge ones," I pointed out. "But we can use them for chairs and a table."

He smiled broadly. "Speaking of which, it's twelve o'clock. How about a pizza?"

"Twelve o' clock?" I started. Angela would be furious! I'd been so involved with the stones, I'd almost forgotten that I'd run away. Would Angela have figured out where I was by now?

"So, how about a pizza?" said Jackson.

My stomach was rumbling.

"Sure, I'll stay for pizza," I said hesitantly. I should have told him then, I suppose, about how I wasn't living at home and about how Angela had said that I couldn't go to my job, but I couldn't bear to bring it up. Knowing Jackson, he would have taken me back to the boarding home right away. It might have meant saying good-bye to him forever.

"What a great job you've done!" Jackson exclaimed, rubbing his hands together. "As far as I can tell, the yard is finished. Maybe you'll come over the day Brielle visits. I'd like for her to meet you."

"I'd like to meet her, too," I said eagerly, "if I can...." My voice trailed off.

Jackson went inside to order the pizza, and I wandered around the yard. It certainly did look different from the day that I'd started! I was glad that Jackson was pleased. I liked it, too, but I still wished that the yard had more color. I peeked into the shed, which was a lot emptier than it had been, now that we'd cleaned it out and the Salvation Army had picked up the things we'd decided to give away. But Brielle's old green tricycle was safe in the back with a few other things that Jackson and I had decided to save. My eye fell on the rainbow-colored hammock, sitting on a shelf. I took it down and hurried across the yard. There was still a hook on the tree and another one on the side of the house! I let the hammock drop open and fastened it up, hooking one end of the rope to the tree and the other end to the house. There were a couple of worn spots in the fabric, but the rainbow colors were wonderful. I sat down in the middle of the hammock to test it. Jackson came out.

"That old thing still works, huh?"

I nodded. "I thought it might come in handy. When Brielle comes, she can take a nap here."

"Why don't you?" Jackson said gently. "There are dark circles under your eyes."

"I am a little pooped," I confessed.

"Stretch out and rest," he encouraged. "I'll wait for the delivery. Would you like a drink?"

"Yes, I'm thirsty," I told him. I glanced at my arms. "I'm filthy dirty, too. I should wash up."

"You can do that later on," said Jackson. "I'll find you something cold in the refrigerator."

He disappeared again. I let my head fall back on the hammock and lifted my legs and stretched them out.

My body relaxed. The leaves on the limbs above created a canopy. I closed my eyes and took a deep breath. I wanted things to be different. To be the daughter of somebody who wasn't crazy, and the sister of somebody who wasn't in trouble. It was selfish, I know. I loved my family, but just for a minute, I wanted to live in Jackson's tall brick house. I know it was only a fairy tale, but instead of being Mistress Haley the Gardener, I wanted to be the princess. Or not the princess at all, because that's not what mattered. I wanted to be Jackson's daughter, like Brielle.

The next thing I knew, Jackson was shaking my arm.

"Haley, get up." I heard his voice as if it were far away. "She's dead to the world."

I opened my eyes. Jackson was standing over me, and Terry was standing next to him! The blood rushed to my head as I tried to get up.

"Hello, Haley," she said. I glanced at Jackson guiltily.

"Why didn't you tell me that you'd been moved to a group boarding home?" Jackson asked.

"I was too busy working," I said, fumbling for an explanation. "They wanted me to quit my job," I blurted out. "It isn't fair!" I climbed out of the hammock and faced Terry.

"You shouldn't have run away," said Terry in a clipped voice. "We could have discussed it."

"Angela didn't want to discuss it," I argued. "What are you going to do?" I muttered sarcastically. "Put me in jail like Otis?"

"No one is going to put you anywhere," said Terry.

"You already have," I cried. "You made me leave my apartment!"

"Why don't we sit down?" Jackson suggested, motioning to the big rocks in the back. "Haley's lunch just arrived. She hasn't eaten."

"I could use that cold drink, too," I griped.

Terry followed Jackson and me to the back of the yard. A pizza box was perched on a rock. Jackson offered me a can of lemonade. I took a big gulp.

"How did you think Angela would feel when she discovered that you'd run away?" Terry asked.

"I didn't run away," I said stubbornly. "I could have. But I didn't. I went to my job."

"You lied to Angela," Terry insisted. "You told her that you worked in Queens."

"Ma knows where I work," I grumbled. "Eventually, you figured it out."

"We tried calling your mother," she said, tapping her foot. "She was having some kind of treatment. She couldn't talk to us until just a little while ago."

"What kind of treatment?" I asked in alarm. "Is she all right?"

"She's fine," Terry assured me. "But she was sick with worry when she found out that you'd disappeared."

"But I didn't disappear!" I said, stamping my foot. "If Ma gets worse, it'll be your fault for telling her."

"Don't you think you're being a little unreasonable?" Terry said impatiently. "You're the one who caused all the trouble, Mahalia."

"I told you I'm sorry! What do you want from me?"

Jackson stepped up and touched my arm. "Why don't you eat your pizza, Haley? I'd like to speak with Terry for a few minutes."

He gave Terry a nod, and they stepped aside and began walking around the yard. I opened the pizza box and grabbed a slice, keeping my eye on them. How was it that some social worker had control over my life all of a sudden? I hoped Jackson was giving her a piece of his mind! I stuffed down my pizza greedily and took another slice. By the time Jackson and Terry were done talking, I'd finished two more slices, and the two of them were smiling. Circling back in my direction, they stopped in front of me.

"Jackson showed me your nice sculptures," Terry announced.

"I made the stone borders, too," I said grudgingly.

She smiled.

"So, what is my fate?" I muttered. "Can I go back to my apartment?"

"I'm afraid not," said Terry. "Until your mother gets well, you're our responsibility. But I'd like for you to keep your summer job."

"Really?" I cried.

Jackson reached for my hand.

"I convinced Terry that you're too good to let go."

I glanced around the yard. "But—but it's all done," I stammered hesitantly.

"Nonsense," said Jackson. "We've got more to do before Brielle comes. We have to go shopping, and we need to fix that leg on the grill. I'll keep you busy."

"I think it's a good idea that you stay on," Terry added. "Your mother told us how important this job with Mr. Jackson is to you."

"She told you that?"

"You seem surprised," Terry remarked.

"Ma is usually so upset. I didn't think she'd remember something like that."

"Everything concerning you is important to her, Mahalia," said Terry. "She just can't show it all the time."

"Maybe I should call her," I said. "She's probably still worried about me."

Jackson, Terry, and I went into the house. I washed my hands and then used the phone. Ma answered right away, but her voice was groggy.

"It's me, Ma."

"Haley...Is that you?"

"Yes, Ma."

"They told me that...you were lost."

"I just went to Jackson's. I'm fine. Terry found me."

"They said you went to Queens. I told them that couldn't be right. I gave them Jackson's name." She spoke so softly. It was hard to hear her.

"You sound tired, Ma."

She sighed. "The doctor did something different. This time it's got to work, Haley. I can't stay here forever, you know. The insurance won't cover it."

Her voice faded away. I held the phone and listened to

her breathing. Deep down, I was hurting. "Should I come and visit you?"

"No. Stay put. Is the place where you're staying all right?"

"I like it okay," I lied. "I'm going back there."

"So, you haven't disappeared?" Her voice drifted off again.

"Don't fade out on me, Ma," I pleaded. "Can I see Otis?"

"No. Your brother is too ashamed."

"Otis doesn't have to be ashamed in front of me."

"I have to go, honey. I can't talk about it."

I let out a breath. "Bye, Ma." Jackson took the phone away and hung it up.

"Ready to go home?" asked Terry.

"Which home?" I sighed.

"Your temporary one," she said cheerfully. "The one with Yvonne, Maria, Angela, and Rayelle."

I rolled my eyes. "Too many new names."

"It's hard," agreed Terry.

"I'd like to come, too," Jackson piped up. He smiled at me warmly.

"How come?" I asked.

He shrugged. "I just want to, that's all. I'll leave a note for my students."

*　　*　　*

When we got back to the apartment, Angela had gone home. Rayelle was in the kitchen folding a pile of clean laundry.

"Here she is," Terry announced, nudging me forward. "We've found Mahalia!"

"Hi, there," Rayelle said. She cocked her head and gave me a look. Instead of being covered with autumn leaves, the dress she wore that day was covered with a ladybug design. "So, you ditched us this morning. How was your trip?" she teased. "Have a safe landing?"

"I guess so," I murmured.

"Welcome back," she said.

"This is Mr. Jackson, Rayelle," Terry continued. "He's Mahalia's employer."

Rayelle and Jackson shook hands.

A girlish voice came out of the bedroom. "Is that you, Mahaley?" Yvonne came running out of the room, with Maria sauntering behind her.

"My name is Mahalia," I said with a laugh. "But most people call me Haley."

"So, where did you go?" Maria asked with a pout. "Angela said you were trying to get to Queens. You should have asked me how to get to Queens. That's where my father lives."

"I didn't go to Queens," I explained. "I went to work." I motioned to Jackson. "This is my boss."

"I thought he was your daddy," Yvonne said.

I shook my head. "My daddy doesn't live around here."

"Mine doesn't, either," Yvonne said softly. "Mine died."

A pang went through my heart. "I'm sorry," I whispered. Jackson grasped my hand.

"So, are you going to show me your room?"

"We'll show you, too," Maria said, leading the way. "It was our bedroom first, you know. Haley just moved in yesterday."

I trudged into the yellow bedroom. Toys were everywhere.

"Looks like you've been playing this afternoon," I said to Yvonne. She ran behind the bed where I'd slept.

"Look, Haley! Look what we found!" She held up my stuffed snake and waved it in the air.

"That's mine!" I shrieked. "Put that down!" I ran behind my bed. The things that I'd brought in my box were scattered everywhere. "What kind of place is this?" I cried. "These things are mine! Who told you that you could bother them?"

"We were only taking a peek at them," said Maria. "Nothing got broken."

"You still shouldn't have messed with my stuff," I hissed, gathering up my books and pajamas. The sock with the earrings in it was under the bed. Jackson knelt down to help me.

"Look who's here," he said, picking up Monkey.

"You told me that I could take Monkey home," I reminded him.

"I remember," he said gently. "I'm so glad you brought Monkey with you." He gave Monkey's head a little stroke and placed him in the box.

"Everything okay in there?" Rayelle called out.

"We're fine," Jackson called back.

I snatched my box, stood up, and put it on the bed.

"We didn't mean to upset you," Maria said, coming up to me. "We were just curious."

"The snake and the monkey are cute," added Yvonne. "What are their names?"

"Snake and Monkey," I said quietly. Maria burst into giggles and so did Yvonne.

I cracked a smile. "Not too original, huh?" I plopped down on the bed next to my box.

"What else do you have in there?" Jackson asked, taking a peek.

"This is my *Grimms'*," I said, pointing to the fairy-tale book.

"And I see you brought the famous thesaurus, of course," Jackson observed.

"This is where I learned the word *discomboomerated*," I boasted, picking up the thesaurus. I swiftly turned to the index. "Hey, I can't find it," I murmured. I turned to the words for *upset*. Where I should have found *discomboomerated* was the word *discombobulated!*

"Guess I made a mistake," I muttered.

"What does discomboomerated mean?" asked Maria.

"It means *this!*" said Yvonne, jumping up and down and beating her chest.

"You're right!" I cried. "And this is what discombobulated is!" I popped up off the bed and began shaking my head furiously and spinning around. Yvonne and Maria began imitating me. We bobbed our heads around like crazy chickens and spun and spun all over the room. Eventually, we all got dizzy and collapsed onto my bed. I was out of breath, and Yvonne and Maria were laughing.

"Bravo!" Jackson said, clapping his hands. "A new kind

of charades! Keep it up. You guys are hysterical!" Yvonne and Maria lay there breathing hard. I heaved a sigh.

"How about if I read everybody a story out of this other book?" he suggested, picking up the *Grimms'*.

"Yes, read one!" cried Yvonne, sitting up. She and Maria drew closer.

"What do you say, Haley?" Jackson asked, glancing at the table of contents. "How about that story about the clever little tailor?"

"Okay," I said.

So Jackson read us the story of the brave little tailor and how he got "seven in one blow." Of course, the tailor had killed seven *flies*, when they landed on his jelly sandwich, but he boasted so much that the world thought that instead of flies, he'd whipped giants. By the end of the story, the tailor did wind up getting the best of two giants and a wild boar. He became a king and a hero, not because he was so strong, but because he was so clever.

Jackson read the tailor's part in a squeaky, high-pitched voice. He read the part of the giant in a low, booming voice. When he finished reading the story, we all clapped. "Thanks," I said, resting my head on his shoulder. "You make it seem real when you read."

"Read us another story!" cried Yvonne.

"I can't," said Jackson. "I have to go." I walked him to the door.

"Will I see you tomorrow, Haley?"

I glanced at Rayelle.

"She'll be there," Rayelle promised.

Just before dinner, Terry came to pick me up. First we went to my apartment, where I got some more clothes. I also got my basketball. We were in and out pretty quickly. The apartment was desolate without Ma and Otis there. Before leaving the building, we knocked on Mrs. Brown's door. She gave me a hug. I was surprised. She'd never shown much affection to me before.

"Nirvana and I were sorry to see that note when we got back from church," Mrs. Brown said kindly. "Somebody telephoned to say that you ran away to Queens. We were real worried."

"I'm okay now," I said.

"She's in good hands," Terry assured her.

I waved good-bye. "Please tell Nirvana I miss her. I'll be back."

After we went to the apartment, Terry took me to a

clinic, where I saw a doctor and had a quick physical. The doctor listened to my heart and my lungs, and while Terry and I waited, she called the clinic where Ma usually took me and checked up on my shots. By the time I got back to the boarding home, I was ready for bed, even though it was still light outside. But first I took a shower and ate dinner with Rayelle, Yvonne, and Maria. Rayelle told me that later on that evening Angela would be coming back in. I snuggled down into my new bed. Yvonne and Maria trundled in and stood next to me.

"How come you're already in bed?" asked Maria.

"I'm tired," I told her.

"Will you read us another story out of your *Grimms'*?" Yvonne asked nicely. I yawned and reached for the book. It opened up to "Darling Roland."

"This is a very scary story," I warned. "It has a severed head in it, and drops of blood that talk."

"Ooh, guts!" cried Maria. "I like that."

Yvonne wrinkled her nose. She didn't look so sure.

"Don't be scared," I said, patting Yvonne's arm. "It has a happy ending."

"Who's Roland?"

"Roland is the one who the girl in the story is waiting

for," I explained. "She runs away with him, but then they get separated. While the girl is waiting for her darling Roland, she turns into a red stone and then into a flower!"

Yvonne's eyes got wider. "What happens then?"

"A shepherd comes along and picks the flower," I said. "He takes it home with him."

Yvonne snuggled up. "How come?"

"The shepherd wants to take care of the flower. Of course, the shepherd doesn't know that the flower is a girl."

"I think that Roland is the daddy," said Yvonne.

"He could be her brother," piped up Maria.

"What's the girl's name?" asked Yvonne.

"She doesn't have a name," I replied.

"Then what's the shepherd's name?" she whined.

"Oh, be quiet," Maria ordered with a huff. "If you keep asking questions, we'll never hear the story."

I rested my eyes on the page and read from the beginning.

CHAPTER NINE

"Hi, Ma."

"Hi, Haley."

"How are you feeling? Better?"

"Yes."

"A lot better?"

"A little better."

"Will you be a lot better soon?"

"I'll try."

"Guess what? Brielle is coming today."

"Who?"

"Brielle, Jackson's daughter. I told you about her."

"That's nice."

"Brielle makes movies. Maybe she'll make one of us."

"That's nice."

"You said that already, Ma."

"So, what else is new?"

"I went to the grocery store for Jackson. He gave me the money. I went shopping for Brielle's barbecue all by myself."

"How did you carry the groceries?"

"In a shopping cart. Jackson stayed at home teaching."

"Um."

"Are you listening?"

"Um."

"I bought hot dogs and hamburgers and veggie burgers. We don't know if Brielle is a vegetarian. Jackson said once upon a time she was, but now she might eat meat. He doesn't know for sure."

"Um."

"Are you listening? I bought chips and lots of junk food, just in case she's a junk-food addict. Ma, did you talk to Otis?"

"He has a trial date."

"That's good. Can I go?"

"No. It's too upsetting."

"No, it isn't. Are you going?"

"I'm not sure. Write Otis a letter, if you want to. Terry has his address."

"Okay. Hey, Ma, can I visit you?"

"Not today."

"When?"

"Speak to Terry first."

"What does Terry know?" I said. "Guess what?"

"Um."

"Did you hear me?"

"Yes."

"I fixed the leg on Jackson's barbecue grill. It saved him buying a new one. I just found a screw and fastened the leg right on. That's all that the grill needed....Hey, Ma, did you pay the rent on our apartment?"

"Through the end of the month."

"What happens after that?"

"I'll take care of it."

"I'm still saving my money, Ma. I didn't pay the electricity bill, because we're not there to use the lights. But I have a lot saved up. So I can help you."

"We'll talk about it when I get home...."

"When exactly will that be?"

"When you least expect."

"Bye, Ma. I miss you."

"Bye, baby."

Dear Otis,

How are you? First of all, it's okay that you didn't want me to visit or even to talk to me. Ma told me that I could write to you. *I should have thought of that myself before, but I didn't have your address. I cannot believe that you and Ma and I all have different addresses now. But not for long, I hope!!!! Good luck at your trial. Ma and Terry say that I cannot come to it. I am going to ask Jackson to take me though, no matter what! I like Terry, but she's extremely strict. I know that you know her, since she is handling our case. She has probably told you (or Ma has told you, I guess) that I am living in a group boarding home, which is an apartment not far from where our real apartment is. Though you probably have received a new toothbrush at your juvenile facility, I brought your green one with me, just in case I was coming to visit you. I forgot my own! Two girls live with me, Yvonne and Maria. Yvonne is the youngest and is very sweet. Maria can be bossy. But not as bossy as you! Ha, ha! Please write back to me. I love you always.*

Sincerely,

Your sister,

Haley

P.S. Although you might be ashamed of what you did, you do not have to be ashamed of who you are.

I mailed my letter to Otis on the way to the swimming pool with Yvonne, Maria, and Angela.

"Do you think he'll answer your letter?" Maria asked thoughtfully.

I crossed my fingers.

I wasn't supposed to show up at Jackson's until the after-noon, on account of Brielle's visit. Her plane was supposed to arrive that morning. She'd have been flying from California all night long. Jackson thought that she might want to rest up before meeting me and having the barbecue. When Yvonne, Maria, and I got back to the apartment after going to the pool, I changed for Jackson's party. Rayelle had ironed a spanking clean blouse for me that I'd brought from home. Ma had gotten the blouse for me to wear in a school chorus concert. It had white lace around the collar. I didn't want to look formal, though, so I also wore my overalls. I couldn't resist putting on Grandma Dora's pearl earrings.

"Do you think they look silly?" I asked Yvonne.

She reached up and touched my face. "You look pretty, Mahaley."

* * *

I could hardly wait to meet Brielle. I imagined that she would be even prettier than her picture and, of course, would be very intelligent, since she was already in college. I hurriedly walked to Jackson's. The weather was perfect for a barbecue. When I got to the house, I stood outside for a minute next to the stone steps. Even though I'd been coming there practically every day for three weeks, I suddenly felt shy. I hoped that Brielle would like me.

I made my way along the side of the house and poked my head around back. The grill was in place, but nobody was there. Glancing up to the second story of the house, I saw that the blinds were down. I stepped toward the glass doors and peered in. In a chair in the corner of the room, Jackson was sitting all by himself. I tapped and he came to the door.

"Am I too early?" I asked. "Where's Brielle?"

Jackson's face sagged. "She didn't make it."

"How come?" I asked in concern. "Did she miss her airplane?"

"No," said Jackson.

"Then where is she?" I insisted.

"Still in California," he said, turning in to the doorway. "She called me about half an hour ago. I didn't think to call and tell you. I'm sorry."

"But why?"

"She just decided not to come," he said in a quiet voice. "For six years, she's refused to visit me. I guess that my daughter hates me, Haley."

"How could anyone hate you?" I said softly.

He patted my arm. "Thanks for all you've done. Now, run along home."

"Which home?"

"The one where you're living," he muttered. "Maybe you can catch the girls and go to the pool."

"I've been to the pool," I told him.

He sighed. "Please go, Haley. I wouldn't be very good company today."

My lip quivered. "So, that's that?"

"I'm afraid so."

"Maybe Brielle will catch a plane tomorrow," I said hopefully.

"There's no point in discussing it," Jackson said.

"I could do some work," I offered.

"There's no work today," he said. He reached into his pocket impatiently. "There's nothing left to do." He handed me some money. "Here, this is what I owe you."

"But it isn't payday," I said hesitantly.

"Take it anyway," said Jackson. "I'll call you tomorrow." He smiled weakly. "I'll see if I can find something else to keep you busy."

I tugged at his elbow as he turned inside. "What are you going to do now?"

"Maybe I'll read the newspaper," he said glumly. "I've cancelled my lessons. Maybe I'll just sit and do nothing."

He went inside and closed the door. I stared at the yard for a moment. I was so disappointed! All that work we'd done for Brielle, and at the last minute she'd decided not to come. Jackson was even more disappointed than I was. I knew that. He hadn't seen his daughter in six whole years! He'd been counting on her visit so much. When he was going inside the house, he looked so dejected. I glanced at the double glass doors. There was no sign of him in the big room. I strolled through the yard, gazing at the stone people. I had built them for Brielle. I'd carried the stones from the pile and made the border for her. Now Brielle wasn't coming. But Jackson *was* there. It was his house. Jackson wasn't going anywhere....

I had money in my pocket, and down the street there was an art supply store. One quick trip and I was back with brushes and tubes of acrylic paint of all colors. I wasn't sure if Jackson was peeking from the window, but he never came out to bother me. I got down on my hands and knees in front of the stone border. I opened up a tube of red paint and squeezed some out onto a stone. I picked up a brush and made a tulip.

I heard the piano coming from inside the house. Jackson was playing! The music was loud! Chords came crashing down so hard, I thought that the piano might break. But after a little while, the music became softer and very sweet. I picked up the pink paint....

I lost track of time. By the time I was done, my knees felt permanently bent from so much kneeling, but I did have a flower garden—with red tulips, pink azaleas, purple petunias, and bright orange sunflowers with deep brown centers! Along the path leading to the glass door were yellow roses with green vines. I almost painted the stone people, but the paint ran out. I was so busy painting, I hadn't noticed that Jackson's playing had stopped. He came outdoors and crouched down beside me.

"Look what you've done!" he breathed. "Mahalia, this is so beautiful!"

"Tulips, petunias, and sunflowers," I pointed out. "The

pink ones are azaleas. I know they grow on bushes, but I painted them anyway. The yellow ones leading up to the glass doors are roses. I'm not much of a painter, but I think they're pretty good!"

He gave me a hug, and I began crying.

"Let it out, Haley," he said. "It's okay to cry."

"I'm not crying for myself," I choked. "I'm crying about you and Brielle."

"Thank you," he said softly. "But you also have some things to cry about."

I began to sob and sob. It was as if something inside me had burst. I cried for Ma and I cried for Otis and I even cried for Dad. Jackson hugged me again and then stepped aside, waiting until I was ready to stop. Tears were rolling down my cheeks and crossing over my nose. Even my chin was dribbling.

Jackson went inside and got some tissues for me. He patted me on the back. "You've been storing that up," he commented.

"I try not to cry too much," I said. "Guess I figured that Ma cried enough for all of us." I wiped my nose.

"People have different reasons for crying. We all have a right to be sad."

"You're pretty sad yourself, aren't you?" I said.

He nodded. "I was really hoping that this time Brielle and I might have a breakthrough."

"Does she really hate you?" I asked. "How can she?"

"She probably doesn't hate me, deep down inside," he said. "But she's very angry."

"Like I was angry with Ma and Otis?"

"Something like that. Only Brielle has been angry with me for a lot longer. I wasn't a very good father. I was so busy when she was a baby. And I was such a rotten husband that her mother had to leave." He hung his head. "I don't know if Brielle will ever forgive me for that."

"You never hit her mother, did you?" I asked quietly.

"No," said Jackson. "But there are other ways to hurt people." I glanced away. "I wanted to be a success. I had tried being an actor and then a musician. Night and day, all I thought about was making it big. When my wife and I closed the little theater that I told you about, I went on the road. I was gone for months at a time."

"You were working hard to make money," I piped up.

He shook his head. "I didn't write or even call much, Haley. I even forgot Brielle's birthday."

"My father never remembers my birthday," I said.

He stroked my head. "There's no excuse for that, not

192

from anybody. I don't know where my mind was," he explained. "I had a great partner in my wife. I had a sweet little girl. They were the ones who left for California, but for Brielle, it was always as if I were the one who left."

"But you didn't leave them," I insisted. "You were working."

"It was more than that," he said firmly. "Brielle and her mother needed me, and I just couldn't be there. I didn't love them enough, Haley."

I gazed into his eyes. They were filled with tears.

"Your students like you a lot," I reminded him.

He chuckled ironically. "I guess I'm not a bad teacher. But I'm older now. I'm more patient. And I never go out on the road," he added, glancing around the yard. "So, maybe I've learned my lesson. But it's a little too late for me with Brielle."

"Maybe someday Brielle will forgive you."

He smiled. "Thanks, Haley. What would I do without you?"

"You're the perfect father for me," I pronounced.

His eyes sparkled. "You're perfect for me, too," he said.

"Don't get me wrong," I said hastily. "I know you can't be my dad. But you've done so much for me. I appreciate it, that's all."

"I'm your friend. That's what friends are for."

"I just wanted to say thanks, that's all." I glanced away shyly.

He patted my hand. "Okay, Friend, so now that we've had our cry, what shall we do?"

"Have a barbecue?"

"Not today," he said, shaking his head. "I'm just not up for it."

"I bought an awful lot of food," I reminded him. "I hope it doesn't go to waste."

Jackson sat down on the hammock. "Maybe we can have it tomorrow."

"Have what? The food or the barbecue?"

"Both," he said.

"Who would we invite?" I asked.

"How about some of your friends?" he suggested.

"I would like to see my friend Nirvana again," I said with excitement. "She could bring her boyfriend, Dill. He knows how to cook hamburgers. He works in a restaurant."

"Let's call them up," Jackson agreed.

"I really think I should invite Yvonne and Maria, too," I added. "They'd like the hammock."

"Angela would probably want to come along with them," Jackson suggested.

"Or Rayelle, if she's working tomorrow afternoon. Terry must come, too."

"We certainly have enough food," Jackson assured me. He stood up and rested his elbow on one of the stone people. "We mustn't forget Mrs. Brown."

"She won't come. Her legs are always hurting her. Or at least she says that they are."

"Why don't you invite her anyway?" said Jackson.

"Can we also invite your students Shari and Win?" I asked.

"Sure, why not? We'll have a great big party." He tapped my nose. "A great big party, just for you!"

"Why?" I asked in bewilderment. "It isn't my birthday."

"When is your birthday?" he asked, strolling through the yard.

"Actually, it was the day I came and sat on your steps and heard you playing the piano," I said, thinking back. "It was the day that we met."

"That recent?" he exclaimed. "Well, I think a belated party might be in order."

"That's okay," I said. "I've had my birthday. Let's just say it's a barbecue."

"All right," said Jackson.

*   *   *

That very afternoon, we made some of our party calls. Mrs. Brown said that she probably couldn't make it, but that she would tell Nirvana. Jackson's students Shari and Win both said that they'd come. The party was set for the following evening. When I got back to the apartment, I asked Angela to come and bring Yvonne and Maria. Angela said she'd tell Rayelle and Terry. I was so excited that I could hardly sleep that night. It was difficult waiting all the next day, too.

I went to Jackson's early so I could help set up. The heat wave had finally broken, so the weather was breezy and cool. I brought the barbecue food outside and put the junk food into bowls. Jackson had set up a folding table next to the shed. We had salad as well as hot dogs and burgers. The flowers I'd painted on the stone border had dried perfectly! We thought that the large stones in the back would be great for seats, along with the hammock and the two beat-up lawn chairs from the shed. Even though I knew it would get messed up right away, I got out the broom and swept the yard. Jackson carried out an ice chest filled with ice and cans of soda. Then he started a fire in the grill that I'd fixed, and the guests began to arrive.

I was so happy to see Nirvana!

"Look at this incredible house," she whispered behind

her hand, trying to control her excitement. She squealed softly. "Look at these weird stone things!"

"They're sculptures," I said.

"Interesting," said Dill. "Very interesting."

Jackson seemed to like Dill and Nirvana right away. Dill instantly offered to cook the burgers.

"My turn to cook," Jackson said, declining Dill's offer. "Your turn to relax and have a good time."

Jackson's students Shari and Win arrived together.

Shari gave me a tape. "It's Mahalia Jackson," she said.

I felt a warm glow inside. "Thanks," I said, putting the tape in my pocket. "I can't wait to hear it."

Win hardly said a thing. But Nirvana certainly noticed him. "What a hunk!" she joked. "And he also sings?"

"He has a great voice," I told her.

Dill grabbed Nirvana's hand and cleared his throat. "Ever heard me sing, baby?"

Yvonne and Maria were among the last to arrive. They came with Rayelle and Terry. At the last minute, Angela hadn't been able to make it. Yvonne discovered Brielle's tutu in the shed, and Jackson said that she could have it. Maria sat down in the hammock right away and ordered Rayelle to swing her.

It was the perfect party! Everyone seemed to be having fun, even Jackson. He hummed a little tune while he cooked the burgers and hot dogs at the grill. The yard was filled with the smell of sizzling barbecue. My mouth watered as I ambled over for a hot dog on a bun and slathered it with spicy mustard. People wandered around, munching and chatting, or they swung in the hammock, or listened to the hip-hop tape that Dill had brought. It was light for a really long time. The sun was fading just a little and the evening star was rising, when the doorbell rang.

"Who could that be?" Jackson sang out, hurrying inside.

My heart began beating faster.

Ma!

I ran to her arms and buried my head in the curve of her neck. She hugged me tight. She was wearing the beautiful soft blue outfit that she wore in my picture! "Surprise!" she whispered. "I went to fetch you at the boarding home, and Angela told me where you were! I even brought a present for Mr. Jackson!"

"What is it?" I asked breathlessly.

A big smile spread across her face. Everything about her was sparkling.

"Flower bulbs! You can plant them in the autumn. They'll grow come springtime, you'll see!"

I dashed over to Jackson and waved Ma's small brown bag of bulbs in his face. "Look, Ma brought flower bulbs! It's never too late for flowers!"

"We have stone flowers, too!" Jackson announced happily. "Exquisite stone flowers!"

"Exquisite," I agreed with a grin, "even though they're make-believe!" I laughed.

Suddenly, Jackson and Ma were shaking hands. "That daughter of yours is very special," Jackson told her.

"I know that," Ma said proudly.

"Come and see what's she's done with the yard," Jackson said, leading her away. "Hurry, before the sun goes down."

I caught Ma's hand as she slipped past me. "I thought you'd be gone forever," I whispered.

She beamed at me. Her eyes were full of joy. "Sometimes three weeks can seem like forever."

But that's not what happened.

Jackson came back with Mrs. Brown. She'd come, after all. "Surprise!" she called out. "I took a taxi!" I waved. She'd brought a box and a big plate of cookies.

I stood at the edge of the yard, watching the parts of my

life come together. Only a few weeks before, I hadn't known Jackson, or Yvonne and Maria, or Rayelle and Terry, or Win and Shari. Now, here we all were, with Nirvana and Dill and Mrs. Brown, having a party in Jackson's yard. Of course, three of the main parts of my life were missing—Ma, Otis, and Dad. Like three big holes in the sky, the hole for Dad much smaller and farther away than the holes for Ma and Otis, near and gaping. It was as if a swift tornado had come and picked my world up and dropped it back down.

And I was still there.

"Haley! Haley!" Jackson was calling. A chocolate cake with candles had been in Mrs. Brown's box! He perched it on top of a stone while everyone gathered around.

"Look at this!" he cried.

A beautiful feeling floated up onside of me.

"Is that for me?"

Jackson smiled and lit the candles.

I hurried across the yard to blow them out.

Sharon Dennis Wyeth grew up in Washington, D.C., and graduated from Anacostia High School. She graduated with honors from Harvard. Among her books are *Something Beautiful*, a Children's Book Council Notable Book and a *Parents* magazine Best Book; *Always My Dad*, a *Reading Rainbow* Book; and *Once on This River*, a New York Public Library choice for one of the Best One Hundred Books of 1998. She also wrote the "Ginger Brown" books. *A Piece of Heaven* brought back memories of children she knew as a family counselor on New York City's Lower East Side. It also reminded her of tough moments in her own childhood when the friendship of her teacher meant so much. She lives in Montclair, New Jersey, with her husband and teenage daughter.